M000314471

Celluloid City

(with drawings by Jim Ringley)

2003

Species

2000

Arts & Letters

(with drawings by Duncan Hannah)

1996

Cameo

1994

Special Capacity

1992

Distinctive Belt

1985

Martian Dawn

Mar

Da

TURTLE POINT PRESS NEW YORK

tian

wn

MICHAEL FRIEDMAN

Copyright © 2006 by Michael Friedman

ISBN 1-885586-44-2 LCCN 2005926844

Grateful acknowledgment is made
to the editors of *The Hat*, in which a
portion of this book first appeared.

Design and composition by
Wilsted & Taylor Publishing Services

Printed in Canada

FOR DIANNE, HENRY AND JOE

Martian Dawn

One

Richard and Julia strolled along Rodeo Drive, monogrammed tote bags in each hand. The sidewalk was crowded, but they hardly seemed to notice. It was a bright, sunny day. Julia was momentarily struck by how beautiful the red awnings of the Beverly Wilshire Hotel looked against the pale, sandblasted façades of the hotel and boutiques.

They returned, exhausted from shopping, to their modernist glass compound nestled in the Hollywood Hills. Sunlight streamed through the glass-walled living room from the Japanese garden. There, Julia felt, they were away from it all—Morty, Mars, everything. It was just Richard and her. Her old life with Angel and the gang seemed like a distant Jacqueline Susann nightmare.

She watched Richard move silently through the house, stopping to rearrange the flowers and pictures. Sometimes, she reflected, he was like a wild animal—a black panther padding through the brush of Equatorial Guinea at dusk.

She knew that Richard was a sucker for her "come-hither" look. Lately he had been like putty in her hands. Because he would do whatever she wanted, she often had to pause to think about what it was she *did* want. And, too often, she didn't know. Did she even want Richard, now that she had him? Why not? He was a handsome movie star with millions of dollars. His intellect was passable.

"Richard," she said.

"Yes, Julia?"

"Come hither," she purred, and motioned with an index finger. She realized there was some truth to the observation Angel had made: Until recently she had been nothing more than a hooker in a plastic dress, taking on all comers at $500 a pop. Old habits die hard, she thought. "You know, Richard, before I met you I was only a cheap hooker in a plastic dress."

Richard smiled. "Not *cheap*," he said.

Julia was aware that Richard was pulling a Pygmalion routine on her, though awkwardly at best. She sort of liked it. He was attempting to teach her about the finer things in life—how to dress, how to eat in fancy restaurants, how to converse with people "in the business"—not realizing that she was already quite advanced in these departments. Though only a high school graduate, she was a voracious reader and had bootstrapped herself quite an education.

Richard had also introduced her to Tibetan Buddhism. Through his fame, he had become friendly with the Dalai Lama. He had his own meditation instructor, with whom he met every afternoon, usually at home but occasionally at a local Buddhist center. He talked of taking Julia to visit a community of Buddhist practitioners in the mountains outside of Boulder, Colorado.

They traveled frequently: Santa Fe for the opera, Aspen to ski, Casa de Campo for golf, St. Barts to relax and unwind, etc. Julia remembered once driving with Richard through New England in the fall to see the leaves. They had stayed overnight at the Red Lion Inn in Stockbridge, a rambling Revolutionary War–era hotel. They drove along Route 7 through West Cornwall, Sheffield, Great Barrington, Stockbridge and Williamstown. She remembered the stunning yellow, red and orange leaves.

She also remembered Hawaii, walking with Richard

on the Big Island through a park known as Observatory Park, perched on a promontory overlooking the ocean. The observatory itself had seemed impossibly small, a white dome on top of a red brick dollhouse. It sat in disuse at the edge of the park.

Richard had pointed to a stand of bamboo nearby. "Do you know why the bamboo is there?"

"No."

He had grabbed her hands and looked into her eyes. "Waiting for the wind to touch it."

When not vacationing or on location filming, they enjoyed staying in for champagne bubble baths or candle-lit dinners. Richard was a fine cook. His specialty was Baked Alaska.

Their social lives and business lives were intertwined. When they did go out, it was usually for a dinner or party given by or for a costar or partner, producer, agent or publicist.

Richard was constantly developing new interests in addition to Buddhism. Currently, he was taking weekly flower-arranging lessons at the Botanic Garden. He was becoming quite good at it.

On a typical morning, Richard, Julia and Jemima, Richard's assistant, worked out with Yoshi, their personal trainer, in the garden. Twice a week, Nigel, the gardener, came by to tend to the lawn, flower beds, trees and shrubbery.

Their lives seemed complete, but if Julia had learned anything from her studies in Tibetan Buddhism, she knew they were also completely empty.

Two

Night was falling in the high desert all around the Biosphere. On a nearby rise, giant cacti were silhouetted against the sparkling blue-black sky. The Biosphere's transparent dome gave off a pale green light.

Dirk was alone in the rainforest biome. Angelfish, parrotfish, triggerfish and others he couldn't identify swam in an oversize aquarium along one wall. He sat in a blue butterfly chair sipping coconut milk through a straw, watching a TV that was perched on a fluted pedestal. Several discarded coconuts were strewn about. The supply of tofu squares had run out. There was a golf match on, but Dirk was hardly paying attention. He was concerned that he and Monica were becoming careless, even brazen. But Monica would not take no for an answer. It was a dicey situation.

At the weekly teleconference with Trout that morning, Dr. Gold had recited a growing list of problems, including insufficient oxygen production and poor crop yields. Also, the water purification system was on the blink.

"Our self-contained, self-sufficient ecosystems appear to be slowing down and approaching stasis," Gold had reported. "It may be that our model for enhancing the possibilities for interplanetary colonization is flawed. The photosynthesis projections, for example, just aren't panning out."

"Yeah, I see what you mean," Trout said. "I'll have a team of scientists on the blower to you ASAP to see what the deal is."

"Also, morale has been suffering," Gold continued, "which has had an adverse effect on productivity."

"I'll get my people from Booz Allen involved too. We've gotta change the prevailing culture that's developed in there. That's how I see it. What else?" Trout said.

"Does anyone else have anything to add?" Gold asked.

No one did. Simon, Samantha, Judy, Dirk and Monica rounded out the team of biospherans sitting sullenly around the conference room table in the Biosphere's teleconference center.

"Well, listen y'all," Trout said, "I have total confidence

we'll get these little kinks worked out. This project is of major-league importance to the future of mankind. The Biosphere is the linchpin of my plan for turning this 400-acre ranch of mine into a high-tech office park. We'll have our own golf course—and a Westin. This is big. Very big. The press has been talkin' all kinds of crap about the Biosphere, but you shouldn't even be reading that stuff. I know it's been rough in there. But we've got to stick it out. We'll have a company retreat to La Quinta when this is over. Keep your chins up. Alright."

Trout's image on the video monitor suddenly went dark.

The meeting had ended, leaving Dirk feeling dispirited. He wondered what had happened to the "city of the future" that Trout had once spoken of in connection with the office park project.

Dirk pictured something along the lines of the futuristic office park on the outskirts of Paris, where he and Monica had once wandered on a grey fall afternoon. Outsize geodesic domes and scaled-down Bauhaus mid-rises: a toy city set in the shadow of the Grande Arche de La Défense. They had taken an elevator to the top of the arch for a Tintin exhibit: darkened galleries with wall-sized, back-lit comic strip panels of Tintin in Tibet.

To his dismay, during the conference call Dirk had noticed Dr. Gold staring at Monica's breasts. What was worse was that Monica was actually flirting with Gold. Right under his nose! He had pretended not to notice.

■

Late that night, Dirk and Monica pulled inflatable dummies out of the bedroom closet and tucked them into their queen-size futon. It was time for a pizza run. Once they were sure the others were asleep in their rooms, they tiptoed to the rear exit and slipped out. There was a full moon. It was a half-hour walk down the blacktop to the Domino's Pizza in a shoppette.

Three

"Morty," Alice said.

Morty had just drifted off into a reverie.

"Oh," he said, suddenly snapping out of it.

"Have you had any dreams?"

"Yeah. I had one last night. A beautiful, charismatic artist had founded an art institute—on Mars. Someplace off the beaten track, anyway. I'm in her painting class. She'd studied with Hans Hofmann and was looking for a change. She's encouraging us to experiment with Surrealist automatism. I want to impress her, but it's not working out. I'm feeling all bollixed up. My painting is crap. I look over at another student's—another guy's—canvas, and *his* painting is remarkable. Grey squiggles on a white background. Surprisingly simple. While looking at, it the teacher comments, 'There is perfect clarity and harmony at work,' or something like that. I'm worried she might stop and examine my painting as she walks around the studio. That's it."

"That's quite a bit," Alice said. "What do you make of it?"

"I'm not sure."

"What about the other student with the remarkable canvas?" Alice asked.

"It all comes so easily for him. You know, that part of the dream reminds me of what a rat race this business is. They're all gonifs. I'm trying to raise enough to get *Martian Dawn* going and make a little something in the process, and these Arab investors—what do they think, I'm a total schmuck? I've gotta put the sheik back in his cage before he walks all over me. This ain't my first dance."

"Of course not," Alice said. "You've produced several successful films."

"That's right."

Morty had been in therapy with Alice for the past two years. Mysterious Alice. He was strangely drawn to her. He couldn't quite explain it.

Alice had agreed to act as a consultant on *Martian Dawn* to help add verisimilitude to scenes involving Richard's character's psychotherapy sessions. Morty was hoping it might bring Alice and him closer together. He pictured long evenings with just the two of them working out scenes, reviewing storyboards, etc. Then maybe he'd wow her with his collection of Indonesian artifacts, including the pieces he'd picked up on his recent buying trip to Sumatra.

Alice had been excited about the movie's premise, as Morty remembered it. She was sensitive, intelligent, wise and, on occasion, quite funny. Did she remind him of someone? His Aunt Bella?

Outside, it was seasonably mild. The curtains were drawn in Alice's dimly lit Arts and Crafts–style office off Beverly Drive. A built-in walnut bookshelf lined one wall, and a colorful Léger print hung on another. The room had a calming effect on Morty.

"What about this charismatic art teacher?" Alice asked.

"I'm not sure."

"You didn't want her to see your painting," she said.

"No."

"What was your painting like? You didn't say."

"It was—all mixed-up. A dense mass of tightly coiled black doodles—almost like something a child might do—against a blue background."

"What would the teacher have thought if she had seen those black doodles?" Alice asked.

"That I was in serious trouble."

"And that made you uncomfortable," Alice said.

"No question," Morty said.

"There's a lot going on in this dream that might help us. Let's think about it some more. But we're out of time for today."

"Are you coming to the party?" Morty asked.

"I don't know if that's such a good idea."

"Yeah, maybe you're right," Morty said disappointedly.

"See you next time," Alice said.

After Morty left, Alice thought about what had just transpired. She did, it was true, find Morty to be an appealing, outsized character—in a little Jewish body! What is this, she said to herself, countertransference?

Four

A blue whale appeared on the screen.

"There's Monstro," said the bartender, pointing to the small portable TV on the bar in front of Cap.

"Are you kidding?" said Cap. "Monstro could use that whale for a toothpick. Bill, you're a good, even great, bartender, but you know shit about whales."

"Nobody's perfect," Bill said.

Cap had been at the bar for about an hour.

"You know, it's only two o'clock. I'd like to go to the beach to do some whale watching," Cap said.

"The only whale watching you're doing is right here on television, my friend," Bill said.

There was a long pause.

"Yeah, I guess you're right. Let me have another spritzer."

Cap watched part of a show about whales as he finished his drink.

"What is it with you and Monstro?" Bill asked. "I'm no

expert, but . . ." He didn't finish his thought. "It's like Ahab and the white whale."

"Ahab was an asshole," Cap said. He shot Bill a withering glance. "Wiseass."

"If I didn't know better, I'd say you were half in love with that whale."

Yet it *was* true, Cap reflected, that he had developed more than a passing interest in Monstro.

"Bill, can I confide in you?"

"Must you?"

"You *are* a bartender, aren't you?"

"I'm a *weird* bartender, not some garden-variety set-'em-up Joe."

"*Please*?"

"Oh, alright."

"You know," Cap deadpanned, "Monstro *is* a very attractive whale. I guess you could say the relationship is — bigger than the both of us."

Bill and Cap broke up laughing.

"Yes," Cap continued, "I can honestly say that I've never felt this way about another whale before . . . Though there *was* this sea lion in Nova Scotia . . ."

"Really?"

"No. Don't be an idiot."

Cap got up and went into the reading room. He sat in a red leather club chair opposite the magnificent picture windows facing Grand Central Station, and let his body go limp.

Two men in grey business suits sat across the room reading newspapers. Cap had been coming to the Yale Club every afternoon for several months now to relax and have a few drinks. He wondered if Monstro was out there, off Montauk, basking in the sun close to shore. Or perhaps to points north, near Nantucket, making for the depths.

Cap had first learned about Monstro in an article in *The New York Observer*. A Park Avenue matron had been keeping a baby whale as a pet on her estate in Quogue. In a digression, the article had mentioned Monstro, who had been found as a baby by a conservationist couple after his mother had been killed by Japanese whalers. The couple had raised Monstro as a pet, but they knew that one day they'd have to let him go back to the ocean.

Someone had made a quasi-documentary film about it, featuring the couple and the full-grown Monstro, but with a stand-in for Monstro as a baby. Cap got choked up just thinking about it: a lone whale, a solitary Romantic spirit, its life turned upside down by an unseen industrial complex intent only on profit and laying waste to the planet. Monstro was destined to roam the sea alone. Unless . . . unless what? Cap thought. Unless, somewhere out there, he hooked up with someone . . . someone . . . at least simpatico.

Just then Bill came in with a phone message for Cap.

"Monte just called. The new issue of *Whale Quarterly* is scheduled to go to press next week, and you were supposed to finish proofreading the galleys yesterday. He wants you to call him."

"Oh boy," Cap said.

"You need to learn how to multitask," Bill said.

"Who asked you?" Cap said.

■

Monstro had built up a good head of steam and was fast approaching Monhegan Island. It was a crisp, clear day. A few sculptural white clouds were fixed high above the horizon. Monstro had been developing a case of cabin fever in the familiar coastal waters in and around the Hamptons, even with the occasional trip to Block Island. He felt he needed to get away and explore, perhaps even venture out to open sea.

He was happy on his own, but he wondered about the couple that had raised him. Though he was getting used to it, it was tough, after a sheltered upbringing, to have to fend for himself.

Five

"Dealer takes two."

Monica discarded two worthless cards and dealt herself two worthless others.

Simon looked at the two cards he'd drawn, which were the two clubs he needed. "The game is five-card draw," he announced excitedly.

"Yeah, yeah," Samantha murmured with evident boredom. "Whatever. Nice poker face."

"Where was I?" Monica asked.

"Dirk was having a crisis," Samantha reminded her.

"Oh yeah, Dirk was having a crisis. About taking a new job. So he went to see a psychic a couple of times."

"No way," Samantha said, while eying her pair of aces.

"Yup. I said, 'Dirk, have you completely lost your mind?'"

"Well, that is kind of kooky," Gold offered. "But changing jobs can be stressful. Were you there for him? Did you provide moral support?"

"No, not really," Monica said matter-of-factly. "How could I help?"

"Have you had any psychic training?" Simon asked.

"Not recently," Monica said.

"Alright, the Dr. Ruth Show is over," Gold said. "Back to the main event."

Now everyone had their cards. Gold bet a dollar, and Samantha saw it. Simon saw Gold's dollar and raised another dollar. Gold tossed a blue chip into the pot, and Samantha, Judy Gold, and Monica folded.

Gold eyed Simon, trying to get a read on him. Simon's stone face told him nothing. "Alright, Steve McQueen. *Mano a mano.* Just the way I like it. Whaddya got?"

"Victory is mine," Simon declared, throwing a flush down on the table.

Gold had kings and eights. He sighed.

"Sweet victory," Simon chuckled, sweeping the chips into a pile in front of him.

"Don't gloat," Samantha said. "Win one hand, and all of a sudden you're a big swinging dick."

Simon shot Samantha a sarcastic half-smile.

Monica passed the deck to Gold, who shuffled, then asked her to cut it.

"What'll it be? Texas Hold'em? Anaconda? Cincinnati?" Gold asked no one in particular. Everyone seemed a little bored, he thought.

The Biosphere teleconference center looked out on the Sonoran desert. The first lights of evening from a couple of ranches and a residential subdivision flickered in the distance.

"How did you and Dirk meet?" Judy asked Monica, picking up the thread from the earlier conversation.

"Do you really care?" Monica asked, looking Judy directly in the eye.

"Passionately," Judy said.

"Wellsir, he was eyeballing me in a gourmet food store. Practically stole the nuts and berries right out of my shopping cart."

"Land sakes," said Samantha in a faux Southern drawl.

"*Something* like that," Simon said. "I think I read about it in the Boulder *Daily Camera*. Wasn't it *you* who shamelessly undressed *him* with your eyes in the aisle? Does hunting him down like a dog in the street sound familiar?"

"Please, sir," Monica said, "you go too far."

"It seems like so long ago," Simon said. "Now you treat him like dirt."

■

Birds twittered and crickets chirped in the evening shadows. Dirk floated on a pink rubber raft in the saltwater ocean biome at the far end of the Biosphere. Johnny Cash moaned on his Walkman:

> *Now she walks these hills in a long black veil*
> *She visits my grave when the night wind wails . . .*

Those lines always got to him. He also liked the part about "the slayer who ran looked a lot like me." He pictured a cemetery at dusk and a young man walking through it.

A voice crackled over his walkie-talkie. He picked it up off his stomach.

"Hello?" he said.

"Dirk, it's me. Come in. Over," Monica said.

"I'm sorry, there's no one here by that name."

"Ha ha."

"What's happening?"

"We're still playing poker. I just wanted to see how you were."

"How do you think I am?"

"Just fine."

"Yes, you're right," Dirk agreed. "Things are perfect."

"I wouldn't say that."

"That's because you have no imagination. Not a scintilla."

"Not even a scintilla?"

"Not a microdot."

"I want a divorce."

"You got it."

"You'll be hearing from my lawyers."

"Always a pleasure."

■

"Did I ever tell you about when I lived in Equatorial Guinea conducting a study on the rainforest?" Gold asked the group.

"I don't think so," Samantha said.

"The prime minister and I became best friends. It's funny, he was only one generation removed from cannibals."

"Oh my god!" Monica exclaimed. "Weren't you worried?"

"Gold's got ice water in his veins," Judy commented sarcastically. "He's a stone killer. Didn't you know?"

Gold ignored Judy and continued. "The prime minister was a spectacular billiards player. He had a pilot's license. He could speak five languages fluently—four of them Indo-European—was a crack shot and could recite Byron's "So We'll Go No More A-Roving" by heart.

As if on cue, Simon suddenly stood up and held forth:

> So we'll go no more a-roving
>   So late into the night,
> Though the heart be still as loving,
>   And the moon be still as bright.
>
> For the sword outwears its sheath,
>   And the soul wears out the breast,
> And the heart must pause to breathe,
>   And Love itself have rest.

Though the night was made for loving,
And the day returns too soon,
Yet we'll go no more a-roving
By the light of the moon.

"*You* were the prime minister of Equatorial Guinea?" Monica asked Simon.

"Simon, you continually amaze me," Gold said.

Six

Hal poked his head inside the trailer. "I've just seen the rushes from this morning and want you to look at the Mars shuttle scene."

"Okay," Richard said, in between swigs of beer. "Can I get you something?"

"Campari and soda," Hal said.

"Coming right up."

Richard's vintage Airstream trailer had been completely refurbished inside. He and Hal sat opposite each other in matching white leather Knoll chairs.

Hal was Richard's kind of director. He wasn't looking for anything fancy. He was content to let Richard do what he did best: be Richard. A writer from *The Hollywood Reporter* had asked Hal about Richard for a story on *Martian Dawn*. "Richard is very . . . Richard," Hal had said. Richard loved that. He *was* very Richard. All he had to do on the big screen was exist: a larger-than-life Richard to the max: china-blue eyes, chiseled chin, etc. Good lighting and the camera would take care of the rest. Richard liked to think of each of his roles as a different "product" in his own personal line. The quintessential Richard character was slippery and unpredictable, but also a master of crocodile tears. When Richard and Julia were cast opposite each other, the audience expected a contemporary, comic spin on *The Naked Kiss*. Richard had to be strong— but also vulnerable.

"Richard, you're like liquid gold," Hal said. "You could be in the worst piece of crap, and just by virtue of your existence, you elevate the entire film to the next level."

"Why *liquid* gold?"

"The camera loves you. But that's what's great about this role—why it was written with you in mind. It's such a *Richard* role."

Richard listed the character's finer points. "Let's see . . . devastating good looks, check; razor-sharp intellect, check."

"See? What'd I tell you!"

"Yeah, but why *liquid* gold? Isn't that oil?"

"No, that's *black* gold."

As a rule, Richard didn't get caught up in the nuances of a screenplay. If a line didn't seem enough like "one of his own," he'd simply demand a rewrite. "I love it. I've come back to Mars for my twenty-fifth college reunion to reclaim Julia, my college sweetheart. I see her from across a crowded ballroom. The room has a 360-degree view, glass floor to glass ceiling. The stars, as well as Earth and Saturn, are visible in the distance. The soundtrack is 'Aquarius' by The Fifth Dimension. I remember the first time I nailed her."

"Very touching."

"So that's how we'll shoot the reunion?" Richard asked hopefully.

"No, it'll be nothing like that, I'm afraid," Hal replied.

"Oh." Richard shrugged. He didn't really care. He was a hired hand. All he could do was sign on with the most experienced director he could, and hope for the best.

There was a knock at the door.

"Yo," Richard yelled.

"Yo, Richard, it's Morty."

"Morty, my man, come in," Richard said.

"I hate to break up this little lovefest," Morty said,

"but I need to talk to you, Richard." He sat down on the couch.

Morty's instincts told him what was up: Hal had been feeding Richard that "liquid gold" shit he fed to all his leads, and generally stroking Richard's ego. "Alright, Richard, you've had your quota of ass-kissing for the day. Good thing I showed up when I did—before Hal blew you."

Richard smiled.

"Very funny," Hal said.

"What's up?" Richard asked.

"Well, for one thing, this trip you have planned to India to see the Dalai Lama—the insurance underwriter is very uncomfortable with the whole thing. And without insurance, our backers are gone. I'm behind you 100 percent. I love the Dalai Lama, terrific guy. By the way, did you see the great piece on him in the new issue of *Tricycle*? Anyway, bottom line, it's a nonstarter. It's gotta wait till the movie's in the can."

"Hmmm," Richard said. "What else?"

"I wangled you and Julia a tour of that Biosphere in Arizona. It's supposed to simulate life on Mars. It's a good marketing opportunity for the movie."

"Cool," Richard said. "Can Julia and I hang out in the Biosphere? To soak up the vibes?"

"I don't know about that. Lemme find out. I'm not sure you wanna do that. I think those geniuses in there are a bunch of nut jobs—kooks."

Richard was only half-listening. The trailer sat in the parking lot of the Griffith Observatory. He was looking south out the window at the Hollywood Hills. He pictured the transparent dome of the Biosphere and, inside, Julia in a white lab coat and tortoise-shell glasses, with her hair in a bun.

"I can talk to Carole Berman about the Biosphere to see what she thinks," Hal interjected.

Morty shot him a nasty look. "Who gives a fuck what Carole Berman thinks," he snapped. "Carole Berman . . ." Morty's expression became thoughtful. "When I hear the name Carole Berman I have to send out a search party to find my pecker . . . It would be a contest as to which would be more gratifying: being blown by her or by Ernest Borgnine."

They all laughed.

"Why is it that whenever you walk through the door,

suddenly everyone's getting their cock sucked?" Hal asked Morty. "It's embarrassing."

"That's a very good question," Morty replied.

■

After they'd left, Richard sat musing in his white chair. Where was Julia? he wondered. Then he remembered she was on location wrapping *Cat Fight at the OK Corral*, the story of supermodels on the loose in Manhattan. What did Julia want from him? She was ... complicated. She had a gorgeous athlete's body, but she could take sex or leave it. She liked to spend lavishly, but her tastes were actually quite simple. He knew that before they'd met she'd led a completely different life, which he could only dimly imagine. Who was this "Angel" to whom she sometimes referred? Latin lover? Hairdresser? Lay analyst? All of these? What did Hal expect of him? How was the plot going to fit around him? And why *liquid* gold?

Seven

"Walter, he is good lover?" Svetlana asked Sylvia.

"I beg your pardon?" Sylvia said. She was annoyed with the turn the conversation had taken, but for Svetlana it was just getting interesting.

"Boris bores me. He is so dull."

"I'm sorry to hear it," Sylvia said.

"How did you and Walter meet? I would like Walter— I mean, I would like to *meet* man *like* Walter."

"Walter and I have known each other forever. We met in Houston. How about you and Boris?" Sylvia didn't trust Svetlana and was reluctant to provide her with anything but the most general information.

Svetlana followed suit and pared her story down to the bone. "I lived in Moscow when I meet Boris. I see what I want—I grab it."

Sylvia nodded.

Kremlin II floated 400 miles above Earth. The titanium skin of the space station stretched over an aluminum frame in the shape of a large glazed doughnut. Sylvia and Svetlana sat across from each other in the galley. Walter was working about 40 yards away, monitoring the core systems. Boris was even further removed, in the tech module, analyzing the day's data from several tests that were being run to determine the ability of various organisms to adjust to life in space. They were all in the middle of a three-month stint aboard Kremlin II.

Svetlana reached over to the intercom on the wall by the table and called the tech module. "Boris?"

"Yes, this is Boris."

"When you are done with highly important task you are doing, do my laundry, please, and then make dinner. I am hungry."

"Yes, Svetlana."

Svetlana turned to Sylvia and smiled. "Boris is good boy."

"Nice," Sylvia observed.

■

Svetlana tiptoed up behind Walter and covered his eyes with her hands. "Guess who," she said.

"Boris, are you up to your old tricks again?" Walter smiled.

"Walter, you make joke."

Walter swiveled around in his chair to face Svetlana. They were alone at the main control panel of the operations room.

"Walter, tell me about your house in Houston." Svetlana pronounced it *Hoo-ston*.

"Well, I've got a condo in a high-rise overlooking a park. Tons of space, open floor plan, great views of the city."

"Sounds very nice. You know, maybe I must be in *Hooston* on business. I could stay in hotel, but is so impersonal. And you have such big place, no? I can stay with you?"

"Uh . . . I'm not sure that's such a good idea. It's just that my place is not really all *that* big . . ."

"I can cook for you. I have written cookbook, *From Borscht to Crêpes Suzette*. You like spaghetti carbonara? Penne with vodka cream sauce? Gnocchi Bolognese?"

Walter listened while he looked out the porthole of the operations center into deep space. He felt it pulling him in. "Well, that does sound tempting, Svetlana, but I'm not sure Sylvia would go for it."

"Who?"

"That's funny," Walter said.

Svetlana put her hand on Walter's thigh. He left it there for a few moments, smiling back at her. Then he removed it.

"Walter, what is wrong?" she asked.

"This is the operations center, Svetlana. I need to keep my head in the game."

"That is what you think. This is sex module. Do not try to fight it, Walter. Do not make me beg."

"Phew! Is it hot in here, or is it just me?" Walter asked, pulling at his collar with his index finger.

"You are helpless to resist. You are in my power. You will do as I say," she cooed.

"Point taken," he murmured.

"I want to be sure. Alright, Walter, I just leave you with something—something to think about."

"I've got a bad feeling about this," Walter said.

She shrugged, then turned and sauntered out, leaving him alone in front of the control panel. What had just happened? Was he developing more than just a passing interest in Svetlana? Were they going to *do* something—sometime soon? And how was her carbonara sauce?

Eight

Monica climbed into bed next to the inflatable dummies, closed her eyes and thought back.

Ten years earlier Dirk and Monica were known as the Archie and Veronica of the MFA program of the Jack Kerouac School of Disembodied Poetics at the Naropa Institute in Boulder. They had met at Alfalfa's Natural Foods during the first week of school. Dirk had felt her giving him the once-over in the fruits and vegetables section. Soon they were inseparable.

They communicated constantly through prototype cell phones.

"Monica, what's your position?"

"I'm leaving the Shambhala Hall and making my way to the parking lot."

"Check. Let's rendezvous at The James at 1300 hours."

"Roger that. Order me an Irish coffee. Over and out."

They both had apartments on the Hill. Dirk spent

most of the week attending literature classes and writing workshops. Monica was studying pre-Columbian art and Balinese dancing. Occasionally, they would drop by the Varsity Townhouses to swim in the pool or would take long walks in the meadow beneath the Flatirons. They spent several evenings a week in the Catacombs bar under the Boulderado Hotel with their Naropa clique. There were plenty of poetry readings at Naropa, Boulder Bookstore or Penny Lane coffee shop.

Monica was fickle, flirtatious, impetuous, unreliable, self-possessed and postadolescent, though a fully developed 21-year-old woman. Dirk was popular with the ladies. His success was due, in no small part, to his dogged determination: He rarely took no for an answer. He was also prone to jealous fits. From the beginning, he sensed that his relationship with Monica was on a precarious footing and that, if someone more exciting came along, she might suddenly break away.

They tried to keep it casual. They might not see each other for a day or two, but as a rule one would usually drop by the other's place and spend the night. Monica was wary about approaching anything even vaguely suggestive of marriage. Dirk, too, was not eager to take the plunge, despite his possessiveness.

■

Monica used to hang out with Simon and Luke. At first, they had seemed a little odd to her. Simon, who'd graduated from Naropa's writing program several years earlier, used a portion of his trust fund to finance the installation of site-specific, abstract sculptures made of brushed steel on his estate-size lot, which abutted the open space along the west edge of town. He would call in the specs by phone from his studio to a metal shop in Denver, where the pieces were fabricated. He had his own publicist and had developed a profile as a local artist, something which in itself was not unimpressive, considering that he had had no formal training and hadn't been to an art museum since he was a young child.

Luke and Simon had gone to prep school together on the East Coast. Luke's wife had bought him a "hippie" candle shop on the Pearl Street Mall. He had two employees and dropped in a couple of times a week to check up on them. He hired someone to redecorate the store, and paid a candle consultant and a retail consultant to prepare a business plan for a boutique candle business. The store had one or two regular customers, and a few walk-ins would come in every week. Luke and his wife lived in a custom home on Flagstaff Mountain just outside of town.

It became apparent to Monica fairly quickly that Simon knew as much about art and Luke as much about the candle business as her Great-Aunt Bessie. Simon's art studio and Luke's store were, essentially, not much more than elaborate stage sets in which very little happened. But she admired their ingenuity: There was a certain Dada genius in the intense focus each of them brought to simply creating and maintaining these façades. They were pretty dopey, it was true, but Monica couldn't help wondering what might happen if each devoted a fraction of those efforts to some kind of serious pursuit. She was certain the thought had never occurred to them. And, far from being oddballs in Boulder, they were fairly typical.

■

Rinpoche was a great Tibetan Buddhist teacher. He lived in a 4,000-square-foot ranch-style house with an indoor basketball half-court in East Boulder along the thirteenth fairway of the Flatirons Golf Course.

To go with his profound state of enlightenment, Rinpoche had a childlike sense of humor and loved practical jokes, the sillier the better. His favorite ploy was to send Blackie Friedlander, the Beat poet who was the director and cofounder of Naropa's Kerouac School, phony letters from young poetry student admirers ("my fellow classmates tell me that I am quite beautiful," "maybe we can meet at Rinpoche's next happy hour," etc.). The letters were full of extravagant praise, not only of Blackie but also of Rinpoche, whom the "student" would claim to have recently met. Rinpoche dictated the letters to his secretary in his office at the Shambhala Center.

He enjoyed entertaining and hosted a happy hour on Friday evenings. He was known for his "world famous" whiskey sours.

■

Richard sat meditating alone in the temple on the top floor of the Shambhala Center, a three-story, nineteenth-century brick building a few blocks from the Hotel Boulderado. The windows provided a view of the rooftops of the city.

Richard had come to Boulder for a weeklong residency in Buddhist studies at the Institute. He was scheduled to give a talk and participate in a panel discussion, and had made an appointment for a private interview with Rinpoche, which was to take place now. Despite his regimen of Buddhist meditation and instruction, he was feeling anxious and wondered whether he was ready.

Rinpoche appeared suddenly in the doorway in an orange sarong, startling Richard.

"Rinpoche, this is a great honor. Thank you for agreeing to this private interview."

"Please don't get up. The pleasure is mine." He looked into Richard's eyes and held his gaze. Then he sat down opposite Richard in front of the large shrine in the center of the room.

Rinpoche proceeded to draw Richard out about his meditation practice. Next he listened to Richard describe some of his concerns and questions. Using some concrete examples from Richard's life, Rinpoche artfully suggested to Richard how he might, in a variety of ways that hadn't previously occurred to him, more easily clear away the confusion of ego in order to glimpse the awakened state.

Richard was deeply moved. He bowed his head and closed his eyes. When he opened them, Rinpoche was gone.

■

Later that afternoon, Monica was checking Richard out from across the pool at the Varsity Townhouses. She was in the shallow end in a lavender bikini. He sat on the edge at the deep end dangling his legs in the water.

She swam over to him. "I really enjoyed your talk yesterday. Tibet must have been incredible." She flashed her best bedroom eyes.

Richard smiled, enjoying the attention but slightly embarrassed by it as well.

■

That night Richard and Monica dined at Laudisio, a hip Italian restaurant located in a strip mall at 28th and Iris.

Afterwards they returned to Richard's apartment at the Varsity.

"What am I going to do with you?" Richard asked no one in particular. He was thinking of a girlfriend back in Los Angeles.

"Oh, I can think of a few things," Monica grinned.

Richard excused himself for a minute, went into the bedroom, undressed and lay down on the bed.

After a few minutes, Monica wondered why he hadn't returned to the living room. "Hey, where'd you go?"

"I'm in the bedroom."

The bedroom was dimly lit. She peered in at the doorway. Her jaw dropped.

■

The next afternoon Monica was just opening the front door to her apartment when the phone rang.

"Monica, it's me," Dirk said.

There was a long pause. "Yes, how may I help you?"

"I'm sorry about our fight—I don't know what I could have been thinking."

"Listen, pal, you're a day late and a dollar short."

"What do you mean?"

"Do you know Richard?"

"Yeah . . . What about him?" Dirk had seen a couple of Richard's movies and was aware he had come to Naropa for a residency.

"I'm with *him* now," Monica said matter-of-factly.

"That's ridiculous. When did you meet him? We only just had our fight the day before yesterday."

"A lot can happen in a day and a half."

"Fucker," Dirk sputtered. "I'll kill him if I see him."

"Always good talking to you, Dirk." Monica hung up.

Richard was the sweetest lover she ever had. She thought wistfully about the night before as she gazed at the Flatirons from her living-room window. A few papier-mâché clouds floated slowly by.

■

Dirk's worst nightmare had come true: Monica had been stolen right out from under him. He rode his bike to campus to see if anyone knew where Richard was, and learned that he was giving a talk outdoors at Boulder Creek, near the public library. He rode there as fast as he could pedal.

Richard had just wrapped up his talk when Dirk arrived.

"Hey, you!" Dirk shouted, jumping off his bike.

"Do I know you?" Richard asked.

Dirk walked up and poked his finger in Richard's chest, then shoved him. Richard shoved back.

"So, this is a fight?" Richard asked.

"You're damn right," Dirk said.

"Why is it a fight? What's your problem?"

"Does the name 'Monica' ring a bell?" Dirk asked.

"Monica? Hmmm ... Brunette? About 5´9˝?" He made an hourglass shape in the air with his hands.

Dirk nodded.

"No, no bells," Richard said, shaking his head.

They stood glaring at each other in the clearing next to the creek. There was silence except for the birds and the gurgling of the creek. It was a Mexican standoff.

Nine

Svetlana sat beautifying herself in front of her minivanity. The full moon glowed in her cabin porthole.

Sylvia was on duty in the operations area. She had left Walter napping in his cabin. Boris continued to compile data in the tech module.

Walter sat wide awake in his bed reading the note that had been slipped under the door.

> *Meet me in Docking Module at 1500.*
> *Dress: casual.*

It had been nearly a week since he and Svetlana had had their first assignation in the docking module. She had told him to be patient and wait for her to contact him when their next opportunity arose. In the meantime, they would go about their duties.

Walter was apprehensive. Svetlana's charms were considerable. Just how smitten was he? He wondered what would happen once they were off the space station and the initial excitement of their liaison had faded. What might their life together be like? Would Svetlana take up golf and round out his weekend foursome at the country club? Would she take to Houston society? Shop at Neiman Marcus? It was hard to say.

When he arrived at the docking module, the lights were dim. It seemed to be empty. Then Svetlana appeared in a silver lamé jumpsuit.

"Walter, you are late! But Svetlana forgives you. Svetlana forgives — but she does not forget!" she said, spanking Walter's behind.

"It's been *too* long," Walter said, moving close and embracing her. "You don't write, you don't call . . . I've been thinking about you."

"I know, Walter. But I have been busy. So much to take care of . . ." She hadn't been busy, and there wasn't much to take care of. The mission was going more smoothly than any of them could have hoped. Her ploy of feigned indifference was designed to pique Walter's imagination, in case he had any thought of ignoring her or fending her off.

"No problem," he said. "Now we're together."

"Walter, what will happen to us when mission is finished? You will return to *Hoo-ston* with Sylvia? Shall I return to Moscow with Boris?"

He smiled and shrugged.

"Well, Walter, I am thinking. We will run away together. Boris and Sylvia will have problems, and I am feeling sad, of course, but there is American expression: Shit happens." She tried to look innocent.

Walter laughed, then caught himself. "Hmmm," he said.

Svetlana studied his face. Could she really rely on him? Eventually, she might get bored with him too. After a brief "honeymoon" phase, Svetlana had lost interest in all her prior lovers. Would it be any different this time?

Walter was developing a cow-eyed look. He wanted to know all about her: her childhood; her past loves; her "lost" years, as she referred to them, on the catwalks of Milan, before she returned to Moscow to train as a cosmonaut. She and Boris had met as trainees in the Russian space program.

"Walter, I have surprise for you."

"I hate surprises," he said under his breath.

"Excuse me, Walter?"

"Yes, Svetlana."

"Oh Walter, you are so funny. I think you will like this," she said. Maybe he will, and maybe he won't, she said to herself. But *she* would like it. "You wait here. I am coming right back."

She disappeared around a corner into an alcove and slipped out of her jumpsuit. Then she lay on her side, resting her head on one elbow, and relaxed. She thought she would build up the suspense by making Walter wait a few extra minutes before making her entrance.

Svetlana loved surprises. She liked to keep her men on their toes, lest they become complacent. It kept things interesting. She would never let a relationship become *too* comfortable. None of her boyfriends had ever known exactly where they stood. Was Walter her boyfriend? Technically, Boris was her boyfriend. The idea of two boyfriends at once pleased her. If only Sylvia were out of the picture. Then how would the arrangement work? She had heard of such situations among the bohemian set in Moscow. Would there be a sign-up sheet? Would each boyfriend be "off" on alternate weeks? No, that sounded so bureaucratic. The ad hoc approach would be preferable. She must think.

Walter had waited long enough, she decided, and she made her final preparation. Then she appeared from out of the shadows looking very pleased with herself, and faced Walter, hands on her hips, wearing only a strap-on dildo. "Walter, you know I only want best for you," she said.

Ten

Richard and Julia sat next to each other in their Gulfstream jet, which Richard had leased. They leveled off to a cruising altitude of 45,000 feet for the two-hour trip to Arizona. Richard was reviewing the week's clippings from the tabloids and other periodicals that mentioned him or Julia. He read that he and Julia were moving to Paris because Julia's dream was to live there. The move was a done deal, he was reported to have said, because his priority was to keep Julia happy. Paris was like no other city in the world, Julia had confided to a close friend. She just wanted to be there, sit in a café, walk down the Champs Elysées, buy perfume.

The tabloids had it backwards, he mused. Julia's carefully cultivated public image was that of a bright-eyed and bushy-tailed floozy with a heart of gold. He was supposedly the more analytical, worldly-wise of the two. Another article had Julia considering a role as a comfort woman in a Japanese POW camp. According to a source, Julia had become fascinated with nineteenth-century captivity narratives and was also considering a script about a white woman taken prisoner by Indians . . . The truth was, Julia was a quick study whose generous physical endowments belied her intelligence. She had a clear-eyed view of human nature, cynical at times, beyond her years. Her occasional temper tantrums were calculated for their dramatic effect. Richard tended to be the sentimental one, always ready to attribute the most altruistic motives to others. In some ways he was quite naïve. Julia, on the other hand, had grown up in the streets and viewed the world with the wariness of an Arab trader in a Middle Eastern marketplace.

He watched her sleeping peacefully in the seat next to him. He found her skin and lashes remarkable and felt compelled to touch her cheek, but didn't want to wake her. She was breathing lightly and looked uncharacteristically vulnerable. Her perfection suggested an air of unreality. Julia's identity, Richard reflected, had in some sense become so fused with her public persona as to be indistinguishable from it. The "real" Julia hardly existed at all.

∎

Further back in the plane sat Morty and Alice. Morty had been having a number of vivid dreams. He kept a note pad on his night table so he could write them down when he woke up. Later, he would discuss them with Alice in their sessions.

In a recent dream, he had fornicated with an old love interest, Bridget Byrne. It was exhilarating. Soon afterwards, his college classics professor appeared as a Monday-morning quarterback and told him to: (1) stick to the text, and (2) not get too excited about Bridget because she'd dump him at the earliest opportunity.

It was a sad litany of dreams with a similar trajectory: utter joy followed by a punishing, humiliating blow. Through his work with Alice, Morty was starting to realize the metaphorical qualities of dreams such as these—that, in a certain way, they reflected his own view of himself. He sensed that part of his work with Alice was the painstakingly slow, almost imperceptible process of internalizing Alice's good opinion of him so that it became part of his own view of himself.

Did he deserve happiness and success? Possibly. But his feelings of inadequacy had been an ongoing problem. Whenever he had his wits about him, he liked to say that he had simply been caught in the act of being himself. At those times, he would try his best to keep out of his own way.

∎

A cloudless blue sky was visible through the dome of the Biosphere.

Richard and Julia had just finished autographing eight-by-ten glossies of themselves to be given out to the biospherans.

"In response to the readings, we can control many variables by artificially adjusting rainfall, temperature, relative humidity and oxygen output," Gold said.

"Yeah, that's interesting," Morty responded, suppressing a yawn.

Richard and Julia were lagging a few paces behind. Julia wished she could simply explore on her own. Richard was content for the time being to blend into the scenery.

"The Biosphere complex measures 20 acres. Essentially, it's a huge, airtight greenhouse. Each of the seven biomes represents a different wilderness ecosystem," Gold continued. "Right now, we're in the coastal fog desert. The vegetation you see around you is typical. We'll also see the rainforest biome and the saltwater ocean biome, which contains well over a million gallons."

"What's in the water?" Richard asked.

"We have porpoises, sea turtles—even a whale," Gold said. "The whale's a recent addition. We'll see how he does."

"Cool," Richard said.

"Such a glorious view." Alice looked outside across the desert.

"Yes," Gold continued, "we get some beautiful sunsets over the Santa Catalina Mountains, and the turtles come up onto the beach."

"Isn't that something. Right up on the beach?" Morty asked with a great show of enthusiasm.

"Uh-huh," Gold responded proudly.

"Wonderful!" Morty bellowed. "But tell me something . . ." he continued, his brow furrowing. "These turtles—will they blow you?"

Gold suddenly looked confused. "Excuse me?"

"Oh, Morty," Alice said. "You never stop." She hit him affectionately with her handbag. "Don't pay any attention to him," she said to Gold.

Richard and Julia were laughing.

"Don't encourage him," Alice said to them.

"I'm sorry," Morty said, with as much contrition as he could muster. "It's the burlesque in my blood. I really am enjoying the tour."

"There are sensors," Gold said, picking up where he had left off, "that monitor light and carbon dioxide."

"So," Richard asked, "the point of all this is to create a self-sufficient environment to facilitate interplanetary colonization?"

"Exactly," Gold said. "Food cultivation and oxygen production are critical to survival—in the Biosphere or on other planets."

"At least one of us is paying attention," Richard said to Morty with a smirk.

"It must be tough," Alice said. "How long has your team been in the Biosphere?"

"The current team has been here for just under a year," Gold responded.

"Wow," Julia said. "How's it going?"

"Well, there are, of course, petty jealousies and squabbles that crop up. It's inevitable: who's not pulling their weight, who's making time with whom, etc. The usual stuff."

"Interesting," Morty said. "Tell us more. It sounds like a big soap opera in here."

"That would be one way of putting it. I have to watch Mrs. Gold like a hawk, for example — can't trust her as far as I can throw her," he deadpanned.

"Alice, you could have a field day in here with these geniuses," Morty said to Alice under his breath.

"Morty, he was kidding," Alice said, laughing.

"Oh really? Too bad. I was looking forward to meeting Mrs. Gold. Thought maybe I'd see if I can still throw the fastball," Morty said.

"Does anyone ever sneak out?" Richard asked.

"Oh no," Gold said, horrified. "Everyone's signed contracts."

They were walking in a circle on a path around the three-acre biome. The ground was hard and dry. There were several stands of small ponderosa and piñon pines.

"What kind of contracts?" Morty asked, his ears pricking up. "Agreements promising not to work for a competing biosphere?" he laughed.

"No, not exactly," Gold said.

"Excuse us for a minute, Dr. Gold," Morty said. "Richard, I've got an idea for a movie."

"Okay," Richard said. "Let's hear it."

"Two competing biospheres: a 'good' biosphere and a 'bad' biosphere," Morty said.

"I like it," Julia said.

"It's the old nature/civilization tension. Works like a charm," Alice said.

"Yeah . . ." Morty said thoughtfully.

They had arrived back at the biome entrance and now stood in front of a bank of video monitors displaying all seven biomes. The biospherans were at work on several screens. A blue whale was swimming alone in the ocean biome. The rainforest biome appeared to be empty.

"We have these displays throughout the Biosphere," Gold said. He took a few minutes to explain the various tasks being carried out by the biospherans and what their typical day consisted of.

Morty noticed that Richard wasn't paying attention to Gold and had instead become fixated on an attractive brunette now appearing on the rainforest monitor. She was brushing her hair while emerging from some very thick undergrowth. "Oh shit," Morty said under his breath. He nudged Alice and whispered, "Code red," nodding in Richard's direction. Alice nodded back.

Morty had enlisted Alice, in her capacity as a consultant on *Martian Dawn*, to help keep an eye on Richard. She and Morty had discussed Richard at length and agreed that it would be wise to make sure he didn't get into any trouble that might sidetrack production.

He took her by the arm, and they retreated about twenty yards so they could have some privacy, while Gold droned on. "I think we've got a situation," Morty said gravely.

"Morty, let's not jump to conclusions," Alice said.

"I smell trouble," Morty said. "Who is that rainforest bimbo? We need to find out. I've seen that look in Richard's eyes before. That was not a look of mild interest—more like an insatiable lion staking out a gazelle."

"'Insatiable lion?'" Alice said, trying to keep from laughing. "Interesting choice of words. Could be you're projecting a little, no?"

"Very funny. Look, Richard needs to be saved from *Richard*," Morty said.

"I agree," Alice said.

"At least until *Martian Dawn*'s in the can. Then he can do whatever the fuck he wants."

They both laughed, then silently rejoined the group. Morty had calmed down and began to focus on Richard more intently. Was he a sex addict in need of professional help? Or was it simply, as Richard had often claimed, that he was catnip to the ladies? The truth was probably somewhere in between. The situation might require some finesse, and Morty would need "plausible deniability" in case Richard figured out what he was up to.

"I thought we'd go to the teleconference center next,"

Gold said, "so you can meet Trout. After that we'll head to the rainforest biome. There should be some good photo ops. Sound okay?"

Everyone nodded. Morty was watching Richard carefully.

"Morty," Richard said.

"Yes," Julia said, laughing.

"Is your name 'Morty'?" Richard asked her.

"No," she said, laughing some more.

"Yes, Richard darling," Morty said impatiently. "What is it?"

"Stop looking at me," Richard said. "I can feel you watching me. You're drilling holes in the back of my head. Would you just calm down?"

"No problem." Morty and Alice exchanged knowing glances.

They all stood on a gentle rise. Before long, a thick fog had descended on the group.

■

Morty had arranged Richard and Julia's tour of the Biosphere to generate some advance publicity for the movie.

A publicist had flown in a photographer and set up some press interviews for later in the day to discuss how the two leads were researching their roles in a simulated Mars environment to bring added authenticity to their portrayals. The combination of Richard and Julia's Hollywood glamour and Trout's Texas oil money had been irresistible, and the press had eagerly signed on.

No sooner were Gold, Richard, Julia, Morty and Alice seated around the conference room table than Trout's image appeared on the screen. He was wearing a ten-gallon hat and a bolo tie, and there was a view of the Houston skyline behind him. "Hi, how y'all doing'?" he asked.

"This is some place you've got here," Richard said. "Thanks for allowing us to visit."

"My pleasure," Trout said. "Morty's an old friend. It's good publicity for us too. Morty, what's happening? How's business?" He didn't wait for a response. "You know what's all the rage in corporate America these days? Started on Wall Street and caught on like wild fire."

"No . . ." Morty said, his interest piqued.

"Janitors insurance." Trout paused dramatically and let his words hang out there for a moment for the group to absorb. Everyone around the table had a puzzled expression. "They also call it 'peasants insurance.' The company gets life insurance on its employees—with the company named as beneficiary. It's a very hot product right now. You ought to think about it, Morty. I can put you in touch with one of the top guys at Prudential who came up with this. Guy's a genius."

"I will," Morty promised.

"How do you like my little theme park, Julia?" he asked.

"It's pretty great," she said.

"It's not perfect—not yet, anyway. But we're working out the kinks. And eventually we'll have our own high-tech office park and golf course. So, tell me about the movie."

"Well," Richard said, "it's the usual boy-girl story. Julia and I do a mating dance, opposites attract, one or possibly both of us turns out to have a heart of gold, etc. Think of it as *Bringing Up Baby* meets *Last Tango in Paris*—on Mars."

"I love it! Something for everyone! It's the American way," Trout boomed.

"That reminds me," Richard said to Morty, "I need to talk to Hal. I'm not sure just what he has in store for me."

"Richard, you worry too much. You're in the hands of an old pro."

"Julia's not old," Richard said.

"Very funny. Relax," Morty said.

■

Alice lingered in the conference room for a few moments after everyone else had left. Outside, the light was fading. She stood by the windows looking out at the desert and distant mountains. She tried to imagine a life of total isolation in the Biosphere and pictured herself and Morty holding daily analytic sessions in an igloo. Had she been watching too many movies? Maybe. Was she losing her professional remove? Quite possibly. Would she, one day, help Morty cut through to his psychic makeup? The odds seemed pretty good. And who was that rainforest bimbo? An owl hooted.

Eleven

"Richard, I've been sitting by the phone these past few years waiting for you to call," Monica laughed.

"I thought you didn't have a phone in here," Richard smiled.

As Monica led Richard to a secluded clearing in the rainforest biome, they began to reminisce.

"I was just a kid then," Monica said.

"You're still a kid, Monica. How'd you end up in here?" he asked.

"It's a long story."

He had a feeling it might be. "Are you still with that creep? The one that tried to clock me at Boulder Creek?"

"*With* is such a relative term, particularly here in the Biosphere," she responded in a world-weary tone. She draped her arms around his neck.

"It's just like old times at Varsity Townhouses," Richard said, gently removing her arms from around him.

"Who's the chick I saw you come in with?" Monica asked. "She looked familiar."

"That's Julia."

"Is she your girlfriend?"

"No, she's my ... psychoanalyst. Can't go anywhere without her. Nerves."

"Oh. Well, do you think your *shrink* would mind if she saw us together?"

"She trained in Vienna. Strict Freudian. She's been a tremendous help to me."

"Lucky you," Monica smirked.

"Don't you know who that is?" Richard asked.

"Yeah. Some second-rate actress."

"*First*-rate, my dear."

"So you're here because you're in a movie together? What's the picture?"

"Takes place on Mars. We're soaking up the vibes."

"Anyway, you're really involved with her?"

"*Involved* is such a relative term—particularly in the movie business."

"You're fucking her, right?"

"Be nice."

"I am nice. I'm just remembering old times—back in the Townhouses. How's your memory?"

"Amnesia."

"So, how'd you meet her?"

"She was turning tricks by the side of the road when I drove by in my Ferrari."

"Sounds romantic. No, really. How'd you two meet?"

"*Really*. You don't believe me?"

"No, of course not."

"So you just stay in the Biosphere all the time?" he asked.

"Yeah, except for my nightly pizza runs," she said.

"Ha ha."

"Hey, kiddo. You ran away." Morty suddenly appeared and put a hand on Richard's shoulder.

Richard introduced Morty to Monica.

"So, how'd you wind up in here?" Morty asked her.

Just then Dirk appeared with a pitcher of iced tea and some glasses.

"This is my fiancé, Dirk," Monica said, introducing everyone.

"Would you all like some iced tea?" Dirk asked.

"Iced tea sounds good," Morty said.

"I'll stick with my Evian," Richard said.

Morty took Richard aside. "It's none of my business, but is everything okay here?" Morty asked gingerly.

"Morty, give me a *little* credit for a modicum of self-control," Richard said. He explained to Morty that he and Monica had met in Boulder and that anything between them was ancient history.

"I'm sorry," Morty said contritely. "I just let my imagination run away with me."

"No problem," Richard said. Then he turned to Monica and Dirk. "You two kids run along."

"But we don't feel like 'running along,' Richard," Dirk said. "Have some iced tea."

"Fuck your iced tea," Richard said.

Monica jumped between them, imploring them sarcastically. "Oh please, boys. Let's not revert to our old roles. Jeez, you guys are so corny. And now we will run along. Take my hand, Dirk. Ta-ta, everybody."

"Ta-ta," Morty called out, waving. "This iced tea is delicious."

Twelve

Monstro swam lazily in the saltwater ocean biome. A couple of terns standing motionless on a white sand beach watched him gliding silently through the water. Judy Gold stood on the beach with her hands on her hips in lime green Lilly Pulitzer clam diggers. The vast scale of the biome dwarfed her.

The scene appeared to Cap to resemble a *tableau vivant*. Was it true? he wondered. Had he found Monstro at last? He peered in from the breezeway outside the biome and noticed that Mrs. Gold was gazing lovingly at Monstro like a doting parent. Monstro was basking in the attention. Cap felt a twinge of jealousy. He was still early for his appointment, so he took out his cell phone and dialed Monte.

"*Whale Quarterly*," Monte said.

"Monte, it's Cap. I'm at the Biosphere."

"Good man. See what you can find out. I love that 'going back to the wild' angle you pitched to me. Maybe Monstro has some dark secret in his past? Skeletons in his closet ... I dunno—maybe he ate somebody and it was hushed up," Monte said.

"He's a blue whale. They eat plankton," Cap said.

"Oh, for chrissakes, I was only joking. But you get the general idea. Have you seen him yet?"

"Just through the glass. My meeting's not for a little while. But I'm sure it's him. He was with Judy Gold. They seem to have some kind of special relationship," Cap said.

"Hmmm ... Maybe we can work on some kind of love triangle angle: 'Monstro: The Whale I Left Behind,'" Monte offered.

"What is this, 'Page Six'?" Cap asked.

"Easy, now. Remember, we need a scoop, the inside story."

"Got it."

"Okay. Good luck," Monte said.

As soon as Monte hung up, Cap placed another call on his speed dial.

"Yale Club," said the receptionist.

"Yes, can you put me through to the bar?" Cap asked.

"Yes sir. Hold for the bar," the receptionist said before patching the call through.

"This is the bar," Bill said.

"Yes ... This is the pro shop calling from Montauk Downs. Did you lose a white golf ball around the eighteenth green?" Cap asked.

"Why, yes. Have you found it?" Bill asked.

"Titleist number 2?"

"That's it. Hey, Cap, where are you?"

"Listen, I've tracked down Monstro. He's in the Biosphere."

There was a long pause on the other end as Bill took this in.

"Bill, are you there?"

"I'm here. Hmmm ... So, you're in Arizona? What are you gonna do? Try an intervention? It'd be more like a jailbreak."

"Whale break."

"Do you need help? I've got people I can call."

"I haven't decided yet what I'm gonna do. I'm on assignment for WQ. Monte sent me."

"Does Monte know about you and Monstro?"

"What's there to know? I've just developed a healthy interest in Monstro. It's perfectly normal."

"Okay, forget that . . . How're you gonna get him out of there?"

"I'm not sure he *wants* to leave. He seems pretty happy. There's a Mrs. Gold here, a scientist, who's all over him like a cheap suit."

"Brazen hussy," Bill said. "What's going on in that Biosphere, anyway? According to *Newsweek*, it sounds like midnight on Monkey Island."

"There's something about this place . . . I can't quite put my finger on it . . ." Cap said.

"Interesting . . . I oughta blow this Popsicle stand and come out there to get a firsthand look. If I like what I see, maybe I'll move in!"

"Hmmm . . ."

"Cap?" Bill said.

"I'm here. Something you said got me thinking. Anyway, I've got to run."

"Okay, bye," Bill said.

■

Cap took in the sprawling Biosphere complex. Then he walked around to the main entrance. Judy Gold was waiting.

"Are you from WQ?" she asked.

"Yes. Cap Martin."

"Nice to meet you. I'm Judy Gold. I thought I'd take you inside the saltwater ocean biome and let you look around for yourself. I'll come get you in half an hour, and I can answer any questions you might have for your article."

"Sounds good." Nice outfit, Cap thought to himself.

They went inside and passed a bank of video monitors. Cap noticed a handsome man who looked familiar—an actor, maybe—and an attractive woman with her hair in a ponytail walking in the rainforest biome. He wondered who they were.

"I'm looking forward to seeing the whale," Cap said.

"Yes, dear Monstro. He's practically family," Judy responded.

So I noticed, Cap thought. He smiled at her, and she smiled back.

She led him down a corridor and directly into the saltwater ocean biome. They stood on the beach watching Monstro, who looked even bigger up close. Monstro stopped swimming and eyed Cap with curiosity.

"Oh, Monstro," Cap said, as soon as Judy had left, "it really *is* you, isn't it?"

Monstro continued to swim, ignoring Cap. He seems to be enjoying himself, Cap thought. Monstro *was*, in fact, quite happy. How he had gotten there was a complicated story. The effort to reacclimate him to the wild in Iceland had been unsuccessful. He had turned up in Norway, after years of being retrained for reentry into his natural habitat. He surprised the Norwegians, who petted and swam with him in the Skaalvik Fiord, about 250 miles northwest of Oslo. Volunteers continued to monitor him. Eventually, it was determined that he was not equipped to fend for himself. He showed little interest in feeding or mating. So the decision was made to find a suitable venue to house him in captivity, since he seemed to prefer humans to other whales.

A few giant sea turtles rested on the beach, while some porpoises swam along with Monstro. The sun was setting. The clouds were pink, with shadows underneath. Cap and Monstro were finally together. The planet had stopped spinning beneath them, and they were frozen in time at the center of the universe. The intensity of the moment was palpable.

They would have no need for society: They would be a world unto themselves. Cap pictured the two of them leading a sublimely solipsistic existence together in the Biosphere, he playing Friday to Monstro's Crusoe. Then the two of them in a shiny stainless steel rocket hurtling through space to explore nearby planets. Cap wanted nothing more than to become lost in something greater than himself.

Monstro continued to swim around, oblivious to Cap, wondering when Mrs. Gold would return. But he half suspected, from the penetrating looks Cap was giving him, that Cap might be involved in some kind of foolishness.

Thirteen

Julia strode to the stage in a gingham Talbots dress, cardigan sweater, saddle shoes, horn-rimmed glasses and a pearl necklace with her hair in a bun. She climbed the stairs, then turned to face the audience and struck a pose: head tossed carelessly to one side, eyes looking knowingly over glasses on end of nose, and hand on hip. Her attitude suggested there might be more to this shy librarian than met the eye. She held her pose until the music began: Marvin Gaye's "Sexual Healing."

She moved with the music, first tentatively, then with feeling. Before long she had let her hair down, stripped to just a G-string and begun to swing her bra over her head with abandon. She grabbed the chrome fireman's pole at one edge of the stage and curled a leg around it, arching her back and throwing back her head dramatically. The Friday night crowd at the Baby Doll Lounge in downtown Phoenix whooped in appreciation.

Angel stood by the bar in a black leather jacket taking it all in. It gave him a charge to see "Esmeralda"—Julia's stage name at the club—turning on the crowd. She had been an exotic dancer at the Baby Doll for the past two years and had spent the better part of the first year as a member of Angel's informal "stable," hooking on the side, out of the club, to support her heroin habit. Their courtship had begun in typical "office" romance fashion with flirtatious banter around the water cooler.

"Hey, Esmeralda, what're you doing this weekend?"

"The name is *Julia*, dick-for-brains. And it's none of your beeswax. I ought to report you for creating a hostile work environment."

"There's probably no such thing as sexual harassment in a topless bar, so I won't lose any sleep over it—*Esmeralda*."

One night he ran into her at a nearby nightspot after the club had closed.

"Excuse me, miss, I'm checking hall passes. Do you have yours?"

"Gosh, I seem to have misplaced it—somewhere or other. Am I in a lot of trouble?"

"You've been very bad. And I probably will have to punish you—at some point. But I think I can let you off with just a slap on the wrist tonight. I just got blown in the bathroom," he announced with a wry smile.

"Let me buy you a drink!" Julia responded, without missing a beat.

"Yes. I'm parched."

They made their way to the bar. Julia wondered, *had* he just been blown in the bathroom? In fact, he'd been making out with a girl at the bar, when the bartender told them to take it to the men's room. They did, and half the bar followed them in, cheering them on. Angel couldn't remember feeling so excited. He thought he now knew what Lee Trevino or Chi Chi Rodriguez must have felt taking the victory walk up the eighteenth fairway.

"I don't mean to toot my own horn, but—"

"Please," Julia interrupted, "by all means, toot away!"

"It really took a lot out of me," he confided, sipping his bourbon.

"I can imagine. You must be exhausted," she said with mock sympathy.

"I think I'm getting a second wind, though."

"Phew. I was worried we might have to carry you out on a stretcher."

"Well, I think I'll be okay. But the crowd, the cheering—it was really all . . . too much . . ."

"Yes . . . too, too much."

They went outside to look at his newly restored black-on-red 1965 Ford Fairlane convertible. It was a clear, starry night. There had been an unpredictable three-ring circus atmosphere to the whole evening so far, and he didn't see any reason why it shouldn't continue. She leaned back against the car. He put his hands around her narrow waist and kissed her.

"Lightning can strike twice," he said.

They both laughed.

"Don't get your hopes up," she said. "Besides, a quiet, romantic night under the stars does nothing for me. I'll take a harshly lit, run-down men's room with a cheering crowd every time."

"Well, to each her own."

He drove her home. She invited him in for a nightcap. Two months later, Julia and her cockatoo, Spanky, moved into Angel's duplex not far from the club.

■

Angel and Julia spent five nights a week at the Baby Doll, which closed at 4 a.m. Their day started when they rolled out of bed each afternoon and headed to the greasy spoon on the corner for breakfast. They spent most afternoons placing bets at the dog track, attending stock-car races at the speedway on the outskirts of town or hanging out at the bar down the block from the Baby Doll with their friends from work. Angel also had a regular Monday-night poker game in his old neighborhood in South Phoenix with an unlikely assortment of drug dealers, pimps, lowriders, thieves, bikers, performance artists and millionaires.

■

As part owner of the Baby Doll, Angel had an intuitive grasp of rudimentary business management principles and did his best to boost morale at the club in an effort to enhance profitability. He gave out an employee-of-the-month award and held periodic contests. The contest for the cutest pet photo had been a big success. He had waged a vigorous telephone campaign among the employees on behalf of his cat, Fluffy.

Angel also enjoyed occasionally taking a few liberties with the truth and creating a little drama at the club as a means of fostering an atmosphere of competition among the girls—and demonstrating his innate sense of right and wrong.

"Hey, Josie, Donna said you don't know how to *do* it. No sense of theater, no foreplay. Just wham-bam-thank-you-ma'am. I said that was *bullshit*. I said, 'Josie can teach you a thing or two, *bitch*. You can't talk about Josie that way. If you persist with these outrageous allegations, it might be best if you were to consider employment at another place of business.'" He noticed the spare wigs on the bar and tried one on. He parted the long red bangs with his fingers so he could see Josie. He looked ridiculous, but, to his surprise, Josie didn't register any reaction.

"Like she's some kind of expert or something. *Puta*," Josie spit.

"Anyway, I just want you to know I stuck up for you, Josie," Angel said, in case his chivalrous role in the scenario he had just invented had been lost on her.

"I know you did, Angel. I appreciate that."

He nodded in approval.

"By the way, you look ridiculous in that wig, Angel," she said. "I'm telling you that as a friend."

■

Julia sat wistfully on a rock in the Japanese garden of Richard's house. She and Angel and Fluffy and Spanky *had* been happy together. And yet . . . and yet what? she wondered. Did Angel really get that blow job in the men's room?

Fourteen

The screen went dark, and the lights in the chic wood-paneled screening room of the smallish production facility on La Cienega suddenly went on. Morty blinked a few times as his eyes adjusted to the light. He rose to his feet and silently stumbled out of the room and into the parking lot outside.

The screening of the rough cut of *Martian Dawn* that Morty had arranged for Alice and him had just ended. Shooting had wrapped two months earlier, and Hal and his postproduction team had recently finished the rough cut. Hal's contractual arrangement with Morty, however, allowed Morty the final cut.

Alice followed Morty outside a few moments later. He seemed to be beside himself. She had never seen him this upset.

"Morty, what's wrong?" she asked. "You look pale. You rushed out without a word. Let's go back inside."

They went back inside and sat down.

"Didn't you see?" he sputtered.

"See what?" she asked.

"The ending is total crap. It's going to have to be completely reshot," he barked.

"What *exactly* is the problem?" Alice asked.

"For one thing, there's no chemistry. And the tone is all off," he sniffed.

"What happened? I thought it was going so well," Alice said.

"So did I. I turn my back on Hal for five fucking minutes, and everything goes to hell in a handbasket. I watched the dailies every day for months, until I was comfortable Hal had everything under control. I hadn't seen any of this footage before," he said.

"Uh-oh," Alice said.

"Uh-oh is right." Morty imagined giving Hal a public dressing-down. In his mind, it was all over but the shouting. Hal was going to have a hard landing. "What was I supposed to do, hold Hal's hand throughout the entire production? It's not his first dance. I just don't know how this could have happened."

"I liked the college reunion scene on Mars," Alice said, trying to cheer Morty up.

"Yeah, that wasn't too bad," Morty admitted. "But the scene where Richard and Julia make love in the Mars Ritz-Carlton falls completely flat."

"Uh-huh," Alice said. "So now what?"

"Well, this could cost a small fortune. We'll have to reshoot the entire ending. The investors are not going to be happy at having to pony up more shekels. But that's life. We'll more than make up for any cost overruns on the foreign rights. It should still be a sweet deal for everyone," Morty said. "Except for one thing."

"What's that?"

"Everyone will have to wait a little longer to get their return. We'll have to change the pro formas. I don't know if we can still make the projected opening date. It's going to be touch and go."

"Doesn't sound so bad," Alice said.

"No, I guess not. I just thought this time it would be different. I need to meet with Hal—alone. I'll break it to Richard and Julia later. I'd like to tear Hal a new one. But this has to be handled in the right way. I need Hal."

"Morty, remember, stay calm," Alice cautioned him.

"Yeah, yeah. I'll say one thing for Hal—he can flush

money down the toilet with the best of them. A real champ."

"Morty," Alice said, reprovingly.

"I know," Morty said, apologetically. Then he looked at his watch. "I'm starving—do you have plans for lunch? I thought we could go to the Ivy."

Alice had been making an effort to keep a professional distance, but Morty sensed that her resolve might be faltering. He was quickly developing a romantic fixation on her. He wondered if any of it was reciprocated.

"Hmmm ... Well, I suppose I could," she said, after some thought.

"Great. I'll call ahead for a table," he said.

They stepped outside the production facility for a second time into the bright afternoon sunlight.

■

Richard and Julia sat reviewing scripts in their sunken living room. Unread scripts were piled in two neat stacks on the coffee table. Discarded scripts had been carelessly tossed on the floor around them.

"You always get the best scripts," Julia complained.

"That's not true," Richard said. "You get good ones too."

"The parts I'm offered are so one-dimensional. I think I have a much broader range. I only need to be given a chance to prove it."

"I think so too. Be patient. Remember, I've been at this a long time. I didn't just start out in roles as a doctor or lawyer or businessman. I only graduated to those kinds of roles after earning my stripes as . . . a gigolo, for example."

"Okay."

"Hang in there."

Just then the phone rang. It was Jemima, Richard's assistant. Richard rattled off a list of midcentury designer chairs he wanted her to look at for the house: Kjaerholm, Bertoia, Jacobsen, Risom, Eames.

"Is anything available in pony skin?" he asked.

"I'm not sure. I'll look into it," Jemima said.

"Okay. Keep me posted. Thanks," Richard said, then hung up. "Julia, I'm going to be in the shrine room meditating for a while," he said.

"Alright. I think I'm going to do some vacuuming."

"Really? Why? Dolores can do it."

"I know. But it's therapeutic — it relaxes me."

He nodded.

"What should we have Dolores make for dinner? Pork tenderloin?" she asked.

"How about grouper with cream sauce?" he responded.

"Fabulous. You know, your tastes are evolving very nicely."

"In tandem with yours."

∎

It was the middle of the night, and Cap was sound asleep. He was talking to Monstro at the mouth of an intracoastal waterway in a "prophetic" dream.

Monstro said, "There's no reason for me to be with you. I'm not that kind of animal — a dog or a cat. Your sentimentality is so hardwired." He was giving Cap a gentle brush-off.

"How can you be so indifferent to something so sincere?" Cap asked from the dock.

Monstro betrayed no emotion. "My indifference is sincere," he said.

■

Morty sat behind his desk in a Century City high-rise. The desk and a built-in credenza behind it were finished in blonde wood in curvy faux Deco. A chrome lamp sat on the desk, and Eggleston photos hung on the walls. Through his windows he had a hazy view of the Hollywood Hills.

"Hal is here to see you," Morty's secretary, Roberta, said over the speakerphone.

"Okay. Send him in."

Hal entered with what Morty, in a moment of irritation, would have called a shit-eating grin.

"Morty, how's tricks?"

"I can't complain," Morty said. He got up from behind his desk to shake hands, and motioned Hal to a brown leather club chair opposite his desk. "Let me show you these photos of the stuff I picked up on my last buying trip to Sumatra." He pulled a heavy green photo album off the bookshelves.

"Wonderful!" Hal said.

Morty sat down in the matching chair next to Hal and

spent a few minutes walking him through the recent additions to his Indonesian collection.

"Just great!" Hal commented, when they'd finished. "Thanks."

"So, what'd you think of the rough cut of *Martian Dawn*?" Hal asked nonchalantly.

"Let me see . . . Oh yeah, I did get a chance to see the rough cut a couple of days ago."

"And?"

"Hal, I'm a big fan of your work. The film is terrific. Maybe your best yet. But the ending . . . it has its moments. I think there's room for improvement."

"Alright, Morty, let's cut to the chase. What'd you really think of the ending?" Hal asked.

"What did *I* really think?"

"Yeah, what did *you*, Morty, really think about the ending?" Hal asked.

"Is there an echo in here? What I *really* think is . . . I haven't seen chemistry like that since Wilbur and Mr. Ed."

"Hilarious," Hal said.

"We're talking big-time chemistry here," Morty continued. "I haven't seen chemistry like that since ... Yogi Bear and Boo Boo. Look, the tone is all off. It's too campy. The first two-thirds of the film have a mercurial feeling. You can't quite tell if it's serious or funny. It's perfect. The ending just falls flat. It needs to be completely reshot."

"Reshot completely?" Hal asked in disbelief.

"*Completely* reshot," Morty said with conviction, looking Hal directly in the eye. "But let me speak to Richard and Julia myself. I know just how to handle this."

Hal left Morty's office with a hangdog look in spite of Morty's reassurance that "we'll nail it this time."

.

Alice shot down Sunset at dusk in her red Mercedes SL convertible on her way to her home in Laurel Canyon. *Morty, what have you gotten me into?* she thought. She could see that the boundaries she had tried to maintain were blurring beyond recognition. The screening and lunch a couple of days earlier had felt a lot like a date. Morty seemed devoted to her. Maybe it would be best if she found him a new analyst to work with. Nothing had happened between them yet. But it might. Did she *want* something to happen? She didn't know. But, she decided, she could not continue as Morty's therapist.

And what about Morty's psychotherapy? He'd certainly made a lot of progress since he'd begun his work with her. He was slowly but surely wrestling his self-destructive impulses into submission. The prostitutes, drugs, alcohol and car wrecks seemed to be a thing of the past. There was something about his nature Alice found appealing, even romantic. She had her own demons, she knew, and perhaps Morty sparked some impulses of her own.

She reached Crescent Heights and turned left into the canyon. She was looking forward to a hot bath and listening to jazz. It would be good to give this Morty dilemma a rest.

Fifteen

The shuttle descended over the vast canyons of the Valles Marineris and then slowed as it approached the passenger terminal on the outskirts of the Mars colony. Inside the craft, Richard and Julia prepared for landing.

The colony was located on the planet's southern hemisphere, where the cratered highlands resembled the surface of the Moon. The complex, which spanned several square miles, consisted of a master-planned, mixed-use grid of geodesic modules. The size and scale of the structures were impressive.

Richard still found it hard to believe that it had already been five years since Mars had first been colonized.

■

Am I my usual self? Richard wondered, after they'd disembarked. He wasn't sure. He couldn't resist gently booting Julia in the butt.

"Richard, you're acting weird," Julia said.

"We *are* on Mars," he shrugged.

They headed for the baggage claim.

When they arrived at the Ritz-Carlton, they checked in and went straight up to their suite. Julia drew a bubble bath, and a few minutes later she slid into the Jacuzzi-style tub, which was now covered in bubbles.

"Richard," she called.

"Yes?"

"What are you doing?"

"Waiting for a streetcar. And putting my things away."

"Come in here—I want to show you something," she cooed.

"Okay," he said, reluctantly.

"And bring a bottle of champagne from the minibar and a couple of champagne flutes."

Richard suddenly stopped unpacking, and his face brightened. "I think I'm starting to feel like my old self again."

A few moments later he entered the white marble bathroom to find Julia luxuriating in the tub.

"Get your ass in here," she commanded, lifting an impossibly long leg out of the water for him to admire, in case he was having any doubts. Some foam fell from her foot.

He slipped in and handed Julia a champagne flute. "To Mars," he said, lifting his glass.

"To Mars. I don't know why we don't come here more often."

Richard settled in at the opposite end of the tub.

"Richard."

"Yes, Julia."

"Come over here," she said and motioned, giving him the look he knew only too well.

He smiled at her as he put his glass down, and she did the same.

∎

That night, Richard, Julia, Morty, Alice, Hal and Carole Berman, the line producer for *Martian Dawn*, met for dinner at the Ritz-Carlton.

"Well, Morty, I hope you're proud of yourself," Julia said, once they were seated.

"Meaning?" Morty asked.

"You've brought us here to the ends of the Earth," she said.

"Ends of Mars," Richard corrected.

"It was a figure of speech," Julia snapped. "Where was I? Oh yeah. Well, I thought the *old* ending to the movie was perfectly fine. So we have to traipse all over the solar system, *Richard*, to reshoot the ending?"

"Yeah, it *is* a bit of a schlep to get to Mars, no question," Morty said. "But you'll be singing a different tune when you're taking champagne bubble baths with the Oscar." He gazed at her pointedly, waiting for his words to hit home.

Julia's face suddenly lit up as she broke into a big smile. Morty folded his arms with a self-satisfied grin.

"I know *I* will," Hal said.

Everybody laughed.

"You'll be printing your own money, Julia," Morty added.

"I hate it when that happens," Richard deadpanned.

"By the way, how come Morty knows so much about my bathing habits, Richard?" Julia asked, with mock annoyance. "I'll speak to you later in private," she scolded.

"Let's face it," Richard said. "Yes, the film's ending did need a little tweaking. But the real reason we're here is so Morty and Alice can do a little therapy on Mars."

Richard could see the wheels turning in Morty's head. Alice blushed and smiled wanly.

"Not a bad idea," Morty said. The thought of it gave him a little charge. Just then he noticed the look that Carole was giving Hal. What was going on *here*? Were they an item? He made a mental note to take this up with Hal later.

"Alright, enough with the jokes, I'm all out of ammunition. Let's order," Morty commanded. "In fact, I'll order for everyone. Let's see . . . Richard, you'll have the . . . swordfish. Julia, the chicken. Alice, the duck. Hal, the goat. And Carole, the—goat cheese salad."

"Morty, I think everyone should decide for themselves," Alice said.

"Oh alright," he said, with feigned exasperation. "I'm too tense. Richard may be on to something. Alice, I think a session on Mars might really do me some good."

"We'll discuss it," Alice said, uncomfortably. "You know, I've 'recused' myself as Morty's analyst."

"Really?" Richard asked. "I didn't realize that. Interesting . . ." He smiled broadly, and nudged Morty with his elbow.

"Morty, I'd like to confide in you. Richard and I took a bubble bath when we got here today," Julia said.

"You're kidding! Well, *that's* a first. I understand it's very relaxing. As a matter of fact, Hal and Carole have been slipping into the bubbles too," Morty quipped.

"Hal and Carole?" Julia asked with interest.

Hal shot Morty a dirty look.

"Morty, you're such a troublemaker," Alice said.

"I know. I can't help it. I just like to stir the pot. Excuse me, everyone," Morty said. "Hal and Carole have an announcement they'd like to make."

"Really?" Julia asked excitedly.

Alice rolled her eyes. Richard braced himself for the worst.

"We do?" Carole asked. "No we don't," she said sharply. "Morty, what *are* you going on about?"

"I thought you and Hal had something you'd like to tell the group," Morty said disingenuously.

"Yes we do," Hal said. He tapped the water glass with his fork. "Friends, Carole and I would like to announce our joint opinion that our producer is a horse's ass."

"You're too kind," Morty said.

The lights in the restaurant dimmed, and it began to fill with people. Through the wraparound windows in the distance, Earth was faintly twinkling.

•

The following morning, everyone met for the first day of reshooting.

The sets were strange and exaggeratedly futuristic, while primitive-looking at the same time: odd, biomorphically shaped rooms resembling caves, with state-of-the-art lighting and electronics. The interiors in the actual Mars colony were, in fact, not much different from some of the more progressive interior design on Earth.

Morty and Hal had dropped by Richard's Gucci minitrailer for a preshoot conference. The trailer was decked out in earth tones and bridle leather.

"You know, Richard, I'm worried about Hal," Morty said.

"You are?" Hal asked, surprised.

"You are?" Richard asked, equally surprised. "I've never known you to give a fuck about anyone—other than yourself."

"Richard, that's unfair," Morty said.

"Unfair—but true," Richard said.

"Well, it's just that Hal's got a lot of balls in the air these days," Morty said.

Richard smiled. "You just want to make sure that Hal's love life doesn't become too big a distraction."

"Exactly," Morty said, giving Hal a pointed look.

Hal, who was nonplussed by this unwanted attention, said nothing.

"Do you want to discuss it?" Morty asked, in his most ingratiating tone.

"No, Morty, I don't want to *discuss* it."

"Now, Hal, Morty has everyone's best interests at heart," Richard said soothingly.

"*What* heart?" Hal said.

"Somebody needs a hug," Richard said.

"Try it, and I'll cold-cock you," Hal said.

∎

That afternoon Morty, Hal and Richard watched the morning's rushes on monitors. Hal had calmed down after Morty promised to "butt out" regarding Hal and Carole. Everyone enjoyed the rushes, but Morty had a little trouble concentrating. He imagined a therapy session on Mars with Alice in the loggia of the Mars Guggenheim on a chaise lounge beneath a Dali or a Tanguy. Just one more session with Alice for old time's sake, he laughed to himself uncomfortably.

·

Alice and Julia sat unwinding in the steam bath of the spa at the Ritz-Carlton. Morty was the topic du jour. Alice tried her best to avoid a breach of professional ethics by keeping her end of the conversation general, but Julia was enjoying the opportunity to play armchair psychologist. Did they come to any conclusions? It was hard to say. Morty was a man of many parts. Steam began to fill the room, and before long everything was completely obscured.

·

Later, Julia browsed alone at Harry Winston. She thought about how each role she played somehow contained a retelling of her story: the woman of questionable virtue making good. There was a lot to be said for branding—and brand loyalty—she reflected. After all, she had something to sell with a proven track record: "Julia."

She stared at the barren landscape through the glass wall.

Sixteen

Svetlana strutted dramatically through the Mars shuttle terminal as though she were back on the runway in Milan. Walter did his best to keep up.

"Walter, you are lagging behind," she complained. "You cannot keep up with Svetlana?"

"Evidently not," Walter responded.

"That is what I like about you, Walter. Always with witty retort."

"I try."

"There is something about this place," she said. "It has very cool, space-age feeling—like Tokyo or Seoul. I feel very *alive* here."

"Yeah, it's pretty hip," Walter agreed.

After picking up their bags they hopped on the monorail into town.

"Boy, I can really use some R&R," Walter said, after they entered their room at the Ritz-Carlton. "Being cooped up on that space station was getting old. No more sneaking around. Free at last."

"Yes," Svetlana chimed in, "we can just be ourselves." She became thoughtful. "You know what Svetelana would like right now?"

Walter tried to read her expression before responding. "I think I have a pretty good idea."

"Oh, Walter, you know Svetlana too well."

"Cherry Seven-Up with lemon?"

"You make joke. No, that is not quite what Svetlana had in mind." She undid his belt, tossed it on the floor and pulled down his zipper. "You would like Svetlana to suck your cock?"

"Well, that sounds like a pleasant way to pass the time."

"Just as I thought," she laughed.

■

Walter was still asleep when Svetlana woke up. She got dressed and went to the lobby to take a look around. She noticed a man looking in the window of Harry Winston. With the notable exception of beady, pig-like eyes, his face was almost handsome. Just then he turned around, smiling at her, aware that she had been watching him.

"Excuse me, miss," the man said. "I could really use some help picking something out. Would you mind terribly?"

Svetlana gave him a noncommittal, measured gaze before walking over to him.

"Hi, I'm Richard," he said. "And you are?"

"Svetlana. I am cosmonaut here for R&R."

"Well, Svetlana, it's very nice to meet you."

The man looked familiar, Svetlana thought, but she couldn't place him. A friend of Boris's? "Do I know you?"

"I don't know. Do you?"

"Hmmm."

"Maybe you've seen one of my movies."

"Yes, yes, I have seen. You are that *guy*," Svetlana said excitedly, as she recognized Richard.

"The very same."

"Why are you here?"

"I'm on location finishing a shoot. In fact, we're having our wrap party next Friday night at seven—in the Metzinger Pavillion at the Guggenheim. You should come."

"Really? I would love to come. Thank you so much."

He said he would put her name on the guest list. "Svetlana" would be enough.

Just then Julia appeared and called to Richard from across the lobby. She eyed Svetlana suspiciously.

"Excuse me, I have to go. See you next Friday," he said cheerfully.

"Goodbye."

"Who's the bimbo?" Julia asked, as soon as Richard had joined her.

"Just a Russian cosmonaut here for R&R."

"Cosmonaut my ass. I can see I'm going to have to keep an eye on you, lover boy," she laughed.

"You have nothing to worry about."

■

Walter sat up in bed. He simply could not get enough of Svetlana and found himself constantly thinking about her. She was so unlike anyone he had ever known—certainly unusual for an astronaut. All that was missing was the sequined bikini and feather boa. And she probably had those in her bag of tricks as well. Then he wondered how Sylvia was faring. O Sylvia! How could he have treated her so shabbily? Had he left her for dead on the breakers? As for Svetlana, he had an uncomfortable feeling. Perhaps his life was about to change dramatically.

∎

Monica, Dirk, Simon, Samantha, Dr. Gold and Mrs. Gold sat around the table in the Biosphere's teleconference center.

"This is a toughie," Gold said. "Because not everyone can go. As you know, we've received invitations to the wrap party—on Mars—for *Martian Dawn*. But two of us have to stay here to keep the Biosphere up and running and monitor the systems until the others get back. I thought we should reach the decision as a group."

"And if we can't reach a consensus?" Samantha asked.

"Then I'll have to make an executive decision," Gold said firmly.

"Uh-oh," Simon muttered under his breath.

The tension in the room was noticeable.

"Well, I think Monica should go so she can rekindle her romance with Richard," Dirk suggested.

Everyone smiled.

"Ha ha," Monica said. "And yet, there is a certain logic to Dirk's suggestion."

"I would, of course, have to go too," Dirk said, "to serve as a chaperone for Monica and Richard."

Gold laughed.

"I can't leave Monstro all alone for that long. He needs me," Judy Gold said.

"What?" Gold snapped. "You've got to be kidding. We won't even be away *that* long. He'll be fine."

"My mind is made up. My baby needs me. My parents left me with a nanny to go skiing in Cortina for two weeks when I was an infant. It was traumatic—I've never quite recovered. Didn't even recognize them when they returned. I promised myself that if I had a child of my own, I would never make the same mistake," Judy said.

Gold started to say that Monstro was not her child, but thought better of it. Monstro might as well have been her child, he thought, so deep did her feelings for the whale run. "I guess it would be a bad idea for me to even consider going without you," he said.

"*Very* bad," Mrs. Gold said, shooting Gold a withering

look. "I'm going to do you a favor. I'm going to pretend that last remark never happened."

"Thank you, dear. Well, I guess that takes care of it. Mrs. Gold and I will be staying here to give Monstro the nurturing he needs. Dirk and Monica and Simon and Samantha, pack your bags," Gold said resignedly. "Mrs. Gold, Monstro and I will hold the fort."

Dirk, Monica, Simon and Samantha all beamed with excitement.

■

Bill sat beneath a large tree on the grounds of the Huntington in Pasadena. He had just viewed the Gainsborough collection. Were the women depicted in those paintings—with bouffant-style hairdos and elegant finery—eighteenth-century drama queens? he wondered. Did the rococo backdrops reflect some inner emotional complexity at odds with the stately bearing of the painter's subjects? He found the women appealing. Then his thoughts turned to Cap, with whom he had recently come to L.A. His relationship with Cap was, he reflected, hard to define: He was part confidant, part shrink, part Boswell.

During Cap's many hours at the Yale Club bar, Bill had

patiently listened to his hopes, dreams and relationship problems, as well as his infatuation with Monstro. His behind-the-scenes guidance had helped Cap navigate the tricky waters of his love life: Precious Flanagan, Molly Schwartz, Erica Wong—the list of girlfriends went on. Bill enjoyed playing savant, and it was true his life was richer for having Cap in it. At the same time, though, he chafed somewhat at what he perceived to be the "second fiddle" aspect of this role. There was something about the sense of living vicariously through Cap's experiences that he resented. Was it even slightly unseemly or voyeuristic? The jury was still out.

Now Bill had written a treatment for a screenplay of the story of Cap and Monstro, which is what had brought the two of them to L.A. He found it curious that all his most vital experiences were somehow mediated, second-hand. Was he consigned forever to play "special guest star" to Cap's "top banana"? Or would he strike out on his own? It was funny, he thought, how Monstro's story—his "captivity narrative"—struck such a deep, resonant chord with him.

■

Svetlana lay on a pink chaise lounge sipping a coconut daiquiri while watching Walter swimming laps in the pool. She was reminded of a photo shoot in Sardinia during her modeling days. Stars and distant planets were visible through the skylight.

"Somebody throw me a towel," Walter called to Svetlana as he climbed out of the pool.

"Walter, I have idea," she announced.

"Should I be worried?"

"Just listen."

"I'm all ears."

"Maybe we don't go to *Hoo-ston*."

"Not go to *Hoo-ston*?"

"Yes. Maybe we just stay here—on Mars."

"In the Ritz-Carlton?"

"No. Condominium."

"Hmmm. You really like it here that much?"

"Yes. There is something about it Svetlana likes very much."

"Well, let's think about it. But you know how you're always changing your mind. You're very fickle, Svetlana."

She laughed. Walter started to think about it himself.

The phrase "Martian fuckfest" echoed through his head as he tried to picture life on the Red Planet with Svetlana.

Later, Svetlana strolled through the lobby and past the shops. Moving to *Hoo-ston* was not a good idea. Walter was becoming so predictable. *Hoo-ston* must be very boring, she speculated. Was their romance losing its magic? What about Boris? She reflected on their years together: training at the cosmonaut institute in Moscow, Moon missions, weekend tennis at his dacha on the Black Sea, etc. Poor Boris. Boris was a good boy. She hoped he would be okay. Did she feel any pangs of guilt? Not really. Then her thoughts turned to the party next week, and she felt a sudden rush of excitement. What about that *guy*? Or would she meet someone new?

∎

Rinpoche entered the lobby of the Ritz-Carlton and approached the front desk. His journey had been tiring, but he had experienced a great sense of peace since arriving on Mars. This must be a very spiritual place, he said to himself.

An hour later, he was sipping a whiskey sour while reading the new issue of *Wallpaper* in the bar of the Ritz-Carlton. The bar, like the Saarinen-style hotel lobby, was all swooping shapes and soaring spaces. The surfaces were covered in carbon fiber and titanium. Rinpoche felt strangely at home on Mars, despite the fact that the Mars colony had no real history or culture. He remembered Blackie Friedlander telling him about how scientists believed that life as we know it had begun eons ago when a large chunk of Mars broke off and became a meteor that struck Earth, introducing Martian microorganisms: the first life on Earth. In a sense, Blackie had explained, we are all Martians.

Seventeen

As Julia hurried by the bar on her way to the shoot, she noticed Rinpoche sitting inside. What was he doing here? she wondered. He was a puzzle.

She slipped quietly onto the set and stood behind Hal, who sat in his director's chair watching Richard hit his marks as the camera rolled. Once each scene was completed to Hal's satisfaction, he calmly gave out precise instructions to the cinematographer and crew for the next scene. It was the last day of shooting, and he wanted to make sure he had some continuity shots in the can to work with before they were done.

During a break in the shooting, Julia spoke to Richard. "You'll never guess who I just saw in the bar at the hotel," she said.

"Who?"

"Rinpoche."

"Really? What's he doing here?"

"I saw a flyer for a talk he's giving at the meditation center this afternoon."

"Wow. We should go. I'm going to call him right now." He picked up a courtesy phone, dialed the hotel and asked to be put through to the bar. When the bartender picked up, Richard described Rinpoche and asked to speak with him.

"Hello," Rinpoche said.

"Sir, it's Richard."

"Richard! Have you come all the way to Mars for my talk?"

"No, not exactly. I'm here on location. We're going to try to make it, though. Listen, I'd like to schedule a follow-up interview with you, if possible, here on Mars."

"Of course."

They scheduled a meeting for the next day, and Richard invited Rinpoche to the party the following week. After hanging up, Richard suddenly remembered how much Rinpoche liked parties.

■

"Well, well. Look what the cat dragged in," Alice cracked when Morty appeared around noon and joined everyone on the set, now in the process of being struck.

"Yeah, yeah, yeah. Out of sight, out of mind. I'm gone for one week and no one even knows who I am anymore," Morty said.

"We missed you terribly," Carole said.

"Thank you, Carole, I appreciate that. I've always said you were terrific."

Morty had just returned from a quick trip to Hollywood to attend the Golden Globe Awards dinner and work the after-party crowd. During his absence, Alice had noticed that she missed him. Or was it just being millions of miles away from home? And what was this business of Morty's about needing a session with her, even though she was no longer his analyst? Perhaps she could find him a referral on Mars.

■

"Svetlana, you are really quite beautiful," Svetlana said to herself, primping and admiring herself in the bathroom mirror, flush with sexual energy. She sized up her breasts as she held them in her hands. She wondered if she would have more sex appeal if they were just a little larger. No, she decided, they were fine just the way they were.

Just then, Walter called out. "What's going on in there? Are you still alive?"

"I'm just getting into shower, Walter, to cool off. You got Svetlana very hot." The shower was filling with steam. She slipped out of her terrycloth robe and stepped in.

Walter lay exhausted on the bed. Svetlana had an insatiable sexual appetite. Sex was almost becoming like work: During each "session," they stripped, and she put him through his paces. If this is what life on Mars with her would be like, he wasn't sure it was for him. He thought back on their affair on the space station. It seemed less like something that had actually happened and more like something that Svetlana had invented. In a sense, he reflected, she *had*.

■

The Buddhist meditation center was located in a medium-sized geodesic dome. Julia and Richard arrived a few minutes before the talk was to begin. The Mars Buddhist community had turned out in full force to hear Rinpoche. A large crowd had gathered inside by the temple doors. Suddenly, the doors were opened and everyone poured in. The center looked like the interior of an actual Tibetan temple that had been painstakingly reassembled on Mars: wood-paneled walls, beamed ceiling painted orange, shrines, altars and ceremonial tapestries and figures. After they'd sat down, it was all Julia could do to stifle a yawn.

The lights dimmed, and then Rinpoche appeared on stage in an orange ceremonial robe, dramatically lit by several spotlights. He made his way to the lectern. The audience was hushed in silence. A purple and white banner with embroidered symbols hung behind him. Then Rinpoche bowed his head.

■

Morty, Alice, Hal and Carole strolled down the main concourse at the center of the Mars colony. Skylights and panels of windows afforded a view of the rest of the brightly lit colony and the dark planet surface beyond.

"What's the name of the place again?" Morty asked.

"Moon Bus Excursions," Alice said.

"Remind me again why we're doing this," Hal said to Carole.

"Because it'll be fun," Carole said. "We can't come all the way to Mars and not do any sightseeing. Don't you want to see the real Mars? Take in some local color?"

"We've shot an entire movie about Mars without taking in any local color, why start now? So, we put on space suits and get to walk through craters?" Morty asked.

"Exactly," Alice said.

"Hmmm," Morty said. "So, it's like a white-water rafting trip?"

"More like one of those double-decker bus tours of Manhattan—but we can get out and look around," Carole said. "There may be a whole busload of new tourists looking to see the real Mars. I think the latest shuttle just landed yesterday."

"Will we see any Martians?" Morty asked.

"Anyone who was born on the Mars colony is, technically, a Martian," Hal said.

■

Julia's mind was wandering. Why was she suddenly thinking about Angel now, on Mars, in the rarefied atmosphere of the temple? Was there something in the air, something more than just the excitement of finishing the production and the anticipation of the wrap party? She watched Richard, who in turn was gazing intently at Rinpoche, hanging on his every word.

"Man has a sense of self which, in his confusion, seems to him to be continuous and solid. The self is, in actuality, transitory. Experience continually threatens to reveal our true, transitory condition to us. It is because we have become so absorbed in our confused view of the world that we consider it real. This struggle to maintain the sense of a solid, continuous self is the action of ego," Rinpoche said.

Eighteen

"The average temperature here on the Red Planet is about negative 55 degrees Centigrade. During the day, in the summer, it's about 27 degrees Centigrade. The surface gravity is lower than that on Earth, and Mars has a very thin atmosphere. In its early history, Mars was more like Earth. The average pressure on Mars is less than 1 percent of Earth's. But it is thick enough to support strong winds and vast dust storms. There are permanent ice caps at both poles. Mars is the fourth planet from the Sun and the seventh-largest. Earth is the third planet from the Sun. Life on Earth began when a Martian meteorite introduced Martian microorganisms. Primitive life may have existed on Mars more than 30 billion years ago."

"Can I get a bite of that?" Morty pleaded.

"A small one," Alice replied, handing him a half-peeled banana.

"Mars has two moons, Phobus and Deimos. They are

closer to their primary planet than any other moons in the solar system. They are so close that they cannot be seen above the horizon from all points on the planet's surface. They rise and set twice each day. There are space stations on each of them, and the very first Mars colony was built on Phobus. These days Phobus has a reputation as a nice spot for weekend getaways and time-shares. Okay. Enjoy the drive. I'll let you know when we get to our destination. We'll be able to get out and walk around and take in the view. But you *must* keep your space suits on at all times." The driver of the moon bus put the microphone down.

"My, *that* was interesting," Alice observed.

"*I* want to go to Phobus for a weekend getaway. Why can't *we* go to Phobus? We never get to go anywhere," Carole joked.

"I hate to see a man henpecked like that," Morty said. "Just take her to Phobus, Hal."

"I may just do that," Hal replied. "By the way, Morty, I really like you in that space suit."

Morty got up out of his seat and, with feigned enthusiasm, modeled it for the group. "I think I may pick up a pair of these moon boots to bring back home."

Hal and Carole nodded approvingly.

Alice started to chuckle. Morty tried to keep a straight face but broke up laughing.

The bus gradually picked up speed as it snaked through the outskirts of the colony in the shadow of curious, spire-like rock formations. Then the grade of the rough dirt road became steeper, and the bus started up some switchbacks. There were several other passengers besides Morty, Alice, Hal and Carole seated together toward the front of the bus. They chatted animatedly. There was also a very good-looking, mysterious man who sat apart from the others at the back of the bus.

"Who's the short dark stranger?" Carole asked Alice.

"I noticed him when we were waiting to put our space suits on," Alice said.

"I think he looks suspicious. I'm going to keep an eye on him. What's a guy like that doing on Mars?" Carole asked. "Though he is kind of handsome."

"Yeah, in a seedy sort of way," Alice said. "Ever had a Latin lover? I did once. Jose Maria. He was a Catalan diplomat from Barcelona."

"Very nice," Carole said.

"It was," Alice said wistfully.

Alice looked across the aisle, where Hal and Morty were sitting, to make sure Morty hadn't heard her. Morty actually had picked up bits and pieces about a Latin lover that had caught his attention. There was still quite a lot about Alice he didn't know, he reflected.

■

When the bus reached the promontory, it came to a stop, and everyone piled out awkwardly in their space suits and moon boots. The lights of the far-off colony were visible in the valley below. The road they had just taken was a black ribbon in the distance. Everyone stood in silence, awed by the vista of the dark, cratered landscape. Alice looked over her shoulder at the short dark stranger, who was now heading back to the bus.

■

The Ritz-Carlton was hopping. The lobby and bar were overflowing with the pre–wrap party crowd. Dirk and Monica sat at the bar, and in a few minutes were joined by Simon and Samantha.

"It's like a Club Med here," Samantha said. "The only money they take are these plastic coins." She tossed one on the bar.

"Looks like a poker chip," Simon said, holding one up to the light between his fingers. "How much is this worth?" he asked, pretending to hide it in his jacket pocket.

"Hey, give me that back," Samantha said.

"I could use a drink," Monica said. "What time does the party begin, anyway?"

"I can't *wait* to see Richard again," Dirk said sarcastically. "Maybe he'll ask me out if I play my cards right."

"He just *might*," Simon offered.

"I'm not sure that I'm at my most beautiful today," Dirk said.

"You mean 'beautificent,' don't you?" Simon asked.

"Yes, yes I do," Dirk said, after having paused for a moment to think.

Samantha and Simon laughed.

"Ha ha," Monica sniffed. Her thoughts turned to Richard. He had more or less given her the brush-off back in the Biosphere. But, she said to herself, hope does spring eternal!

"Simon, should I wear my black cat suit or my black strapless?" Dirk asked.

"Boy . . ." Simon said. "Richard is so finicky. It's hard to know which one he'd like better."

Samantha chuckled. Monica fumed. "I hope you two are amusing yourselves," she said finally.

"Maybe the cat suit," Simon said, pretending not to have heard Monica.

"Yeah, I think the cat suit," Dirk said.

"Meow!" Simon growled.

They all laughed. Even Monica, despite herself.

■

At the other end of the Ritz-Carlton complex, Morty sat in a chair by a poolside table. Alice was reclining next to him in a chaise lounge. They were both facing the pool.

"What was your childhood like?" Morty asked, idly.

"Excuse me?" Alice said, caught up short by the question. "What is this, a session? Are you trying to analyze me?"

"Uh, no, not at all," Morty said sheepishly. "I'm just curious."

"Uh-huh. Well, the truth of the matter is, it doesn't really matter what your childhood was like after about the age of five. Your story is pretty much etched in stone by then. And I can't remember back *that* far."

"Hmmm. Okay." Morty scribbled a few notes on his pad.

"What did you just write down? Let me see that pad," Alice said sharply.

"It's just a to-do list. Nothing to do with you. You just reminded me of something."

"Oh really? Read me some entries from this 'to-do list.'"

"Okay." Morty picked up the pad and read: " 'Secure rights to update of *Le Morte d'Arthur*. Call landscaper.' Satisfied?"

"Yes. Where was I? Having said all that, my perception is that my mother was a bit self-absorbed and emotionally distant. And my father was a bit unstable emotionally. So, it was probably not the ideal environment."

"Uh-huh." Morty's expression betrayed no emotion.

"You know, Morty, if you're going to play shrink, it's okay to show some emotion. That stone-faced approach is old hat. No one does that anymore."

"I don't know what you're talking about. No one's trying to play analyst."

"Whatever. I'm just trying to help you out. You want to know about my recent dreams, I suppose?"

"Well, now that you mention it."

"Not a chance."

"Okay, it was just a thought."

"I've already had years of analysis—as part of my training."

"Oh really? I didn't know that."

"Turnabout is fair play. I think it's very interesting that you would like to play analyst to my patient. It says something very positive, I think, about—your own feelings about yourself."

Morty smiled nervously, then reached out for his glass of ginger ale.

Nineteen

Angel entered the Metzinger Pavilion of the Mars Guggenheim, where the wrap party was now in full swing, and scanned the crowd.

"Look, it's the Short Dark Stranger," Carole said to Alice, nodding in Angel's direction.

"So it is," Alice said, sipping her champagne. "I think he's looking for someone."

"I didn't realize I'd made that big of an impression on the moon bus," Carole joked, pretending to preen.

From across the room, Svetlana was eyeing Angel. Who was *this* cute man? she asked herself.

■

From the balcony, Morty and Hal surveyed the scene in the loggia below. Everybody was there: Richard, Julia, Alice, Carole, Rinpoche, Monica and some of the other biospherans, Morty's Saudi investors, the rest of the cast and crew and many local guests.

"Hal, my man, you did it!" Morty said.

"*We* did it," Hal corrected him.

"Yep."

One of Morty's principal investors climbed the stairs and embraced Morty.

"Morty, you are the man," he said enthusiastically.

"No, *you're* the man, Ali. We couldn't have done it without you," Morty said.

Morty allowed himself to savor a brief moment of exhilaration. Then his thoughts turned to his next deal: remaking *The Fountainhead* with Richard and Julia.

"Ali, I've got a new deal for you," Morty said.

"Oh really? TCB!" Ali said, impressed.

"That's right, Taking Care of Business," Morty said. "Are you an Elvis fan?"

"Oh yes. *TCB* with a lightning bolt was emblazoned on the King's signet ring and on the tail of his private plane," Ali said.

"The *Lisa Marie*," Morty confirmed. "Have you been to Graceland?"

"Oh yes. I have been twice. I like Graceland very much. There are many good old Teddy Boys there visiting with their families. I picked up a limited edition *Speedway* plate on my last visit. So, what is this new deal? How is it looking for *Martian Dawn*?"

"The advance buzz on *Martian Dawn* is terrific. You and your partners will come out smelling like roses. As for the new deal, I'll get you some pro formas to look at. It'll be a home run. Both Richard and Julia have committed. I'd like you and your people to provide not just equity but also mezzanine financing."

"I think I can interest them. They are always looking for someplace to park their funds where they can realize a good return."

"Sounds good," Morty said.

Morty watched Alice talking to Carole. Would the evening turn into a "night of magic" for him and Alice? He wondered.

■

Rinpoche was holding court by the bar at the party in the Guggenheim. Simon, Samantha, Dirk and several *Martian Dawn* cast members were listening attentively as he discussed the ancient Buddhist story of Marpa. "It is only at the point when you have completely let go of all expectations that your expectations will be realized. It is really counterintuitive," he concluded, taking a sip of his whiskey sour.

■

Waiters and waitresses cruised through the Guggenheim galleries with hors d'oeuvres and champagne. Monica was wandering around the party when she spotted Richard in one of the galleries and sneaked up behind him. Partygoers mingled nearby. Large photographs depicting scale models of suburban houses, cars and families hung on the walls.

"Nice party," she said.

He turned around. "Monica! Wow! Where's the rest of your crew?"

"They're probably around here somewhere."

"I love your cat suit!"

"Thanks. So you must be happy your movie's done. Congratulations!"

"I am. It'll be nice to get home. What about you? Back to the Biosphere?"

"I'm not so sure about that. I'm having some mixed feelings about the Biosphere. It's really not working out."

Where was Julia? Richard wondered.

"Look, there's Rinpoche," Monica said, in disbelief. She hadn't seen the great teacher since she'd left Boulder.

"Rinpoche, welcome!" Richard said.

Rinpoche entered the gallery with his group from the bar. Dirk eyed Richard suspiciously, but Richard ignored him and started a conversation with his guru.

■

Svetlana and Angel had been talking for some time. They were drawn to each other. Would they stay together on Mars? Go into business together? All seemed possible. She grabbed his hand and led him into a deserted gallery at the edge of the party. Dream drawings in charcoal rendered in a comic-book style hung on the walls.

As Svetlana held his hand, Angel reflected on the scene that had unfolded between Julia and him at the party not 20 minutes previous. Julia was a star. The dramatic "confrontation" with her he'd imagined had been, in actuality, less than he'd hoped. As he'd listened to her, it occurred to him that her new life was completely alien to him. Suddenly his burning desire to get back together with her seemed puzzling. Had he ever really known her? It seemed to him it wasn't Julia as much as the *idea* of Julia he had been so taken with after all. It was an epiphany.

∎

Alice watched the group that had formed on the balcony around Morty. Was the movie really done? she asked herself. It was hard to believe. Where would things lead with Morty now that her consulting work was at an end? She was beginning to feel tipsy. How many glasses of champagne had she had? She'd lost count. Would Morty try to "have his way with her"? Just then Julia appeared at her elbow looking upset.

"I think I need professional help," Julia frowned.

"My professional hat is down around my eyes," Alice said.

"More like your ankles."

Alice looked around. "The Mars Guggenheim ... What's so 'Martian' about this place, anyway?"

"Nothing. We could be anywhere."

"The Javits Center," Alice offered.

"Or the Kansas City stockyards ... Alice, what's gotten into you?"

"I don't know."

"*I'm* confused—I'm in a state."

"So am I," Alice said.

"We're in this together," Julia said. "Can I tell you all my problems?"

"Sure, why not? The *short* version. I need time to get ready. I think I may do a 'fan dance' later for Morty in my room."

"Good idea. It's a great ice-breaker."

"So, what's going on?" Alice asked.

"Someone from my past has unexpectedly appeared and stirred up old feelings."

■

Richard joined Morty on the balcony.

"Richard, we had a situation, but everything's under control. A gate-crasher—an old flame of Julia's, apparently," Morty said.

"Who?"

"Some guy named Angel."

"Angel? On Mars? What's he doing here?" Richard said with concern.

"I don't know. I think he came with some idea of 're-claiming' Julia. But he seems to have lost heart. Julia's a little shaken up by the whole thing."

"How do you know all this?"

"Julia told Alice."

"Where is he now? I can see Julia right over there."

"Seems he's gone off with some cosmonaut chick he met at the party."

"You're kidding! Svetlana?"

"I dunno. Some Russian fox."

Richard made an hourglass shape in the air with his hands.

Morty nodded.

Richard felt an uncomfortable mix of relief, jealousy

and confusion as he watched Julia below in the loggia and pictured a mysterious "Angel" and Svetlana off alone together in the shadows.

■

"You like Mars?" Svetlana said coyly, flashing a smile.

"I like what I've seen of it," Angel said, giving her a once-over.

"Svetlana was talking about planet."

"Oh."

Walter had left that afternoon for *Hoo-ston*. She was to follow him there next week. But something told Svetlana she would not be going to *Hoo-ston* next week after all.

■

Julia collapsed on a Barcelona chair in the museum lobby, emotionally drained. Angel's appearance, Mars, finishing production, the wrap party—it was more than she could handle. Above the transparent dome of the pavilion the stars were pinholes in carbon paper.

Twenty

Morty had slept fitfully. He sat up in bed in his rambling Coldwater Canyon Tudor and stretched. Morning sunlight streamed in through the windows. Then he remembered he wasn't alone and looked at the other side of the bed, where Alice was sound asleep. He stood over her like Cocteau's Death standing over Orpheus.

A little while later they were sitting on the flagstone terrace having coffee and reading the *Los Angeles Times*. Hummingbirds twittered around the rose bushes. Morty reflected that he was as happy as he'd ever been. Was it too good to be true? He watched Alice carefully reading the paper. Their relationship was still new, and they were just getting to know each other's little idiosyncrasies. They had been spending many evenings at home watching videos from Morty's large collection. Alice had not been overly enamored of Morty's selection from the night before.

"You know what the difference between us is?" Alice said thoughtfully, looking up from the paper.

"No."

"*I* like character-driven movies. *You* like movies about flying dragons."

They both laughed.

"I'm speechless," Morty said.

"The truth hurts. By the way, was I snoring last night?" Alice asked.

"Like a pig," Morty joked. "I was too polite to say anything."

Alice was happy too.

∎

Was Angel her beautiful sex slave? Svetlana wondered. Where did she come up with such ridiculous ideas? But why not? And whatever happened to that *guy*? The actor from Mars. Maybe their paths would cross again . . . She tried to picture Angel's club in Phoenix, the Baby Doll, that he had told her so much about. She imagined taking to the stage and doing a striptease. She had no illusions. It would take some practice. But she was certain she'd be a natural once she got the hang of it. It was too bad, she thought, that she was staying on Mars and would never get the chance to find out.

She watched Angel sleeping silently beside her in their new Mars condominium. Outside the bedroom window, she could see the Ritz-Carlton, the lights of the colony and the desolate landscape beyond. How strange, she thought, that she should end up on Mars. Was it impetuous? No more so than anything else she'd ever done. Angel seemed different from the other men in her life. She had never been truly happy on Earth. Would she find the happiness that had eluded her here on Mars—with Angel?

She had gathered that another woman had brought him to Mars. Apparently, this other woman's charms had been no match for her own. Angel had dropped the woman like a hot potato when he'd met Svetlana, though there had been some mention of a reconciliation.

■

Richard stared out at the Hollywood Hills from the conference room in Morty's Century City offices.

"So, tell me all about it," Richard smiled.

"It's a remake of *The Fountainhead*," Morty said, pausing for dramatic effect.

"*The Fountainhead!*" Richard said, his expression brightening.

"You're made for this role. It's got *you* written all over it. I'm not sure there's anyone else with the size to pull it off and fill Coop's shoes—and make the role their own."

Richard luxuriated in the glow of Morty's praise.

"Who are you thinking of for the female lead?" Richard asked.

"Who else? Julia, of course."

"Julia?" Richard asked, after a long pause.

"You and Julia together are like money in the bank. We can get all the financing we need to green-light any project."

"I've got the juice to open a film without Julia."

"No question. But the two of you together are a huge draw. Remember, we need Saudi money, not just studio money. The Saudis are conservative. I promised them you *and* Julia."

"I hear you. But I think it would be a mistake for me to

keep playing opposite Julia in every picture. I'm a serious actor. I've got my image to worry about. It's an unnecessary distraction."

"How so?"

"Well, the movie becomes the Richard and Julia show—a kind of sequel to the last mating dance we performed on-screen."

"You know, Boo Boo was devastated when Yogi Bear broke up their act."

"Very funny. I think *Boo Boo* will understand." Richard laughed uneasily. Privately, he had his doubts.

"Hmmm." Morty decided to back off for the time being. "Well, just out of curiosity, who'd you rather see in the role?"

Richard didn't know. But an involuntary smile came to his face as he considered the possibilities.

■

Dr. Gold sat in the Phoenix Sheraton with his head in his hands.

"Good Lord, Harold, pull yourself together. It's not the end of the world," Judy said sharply.

Bacteria had been discovered in the Biosphere fertilizer, something that turned out to be the cause of the deficient oxygen production that had plagued the Biosphere almost from the beginning. Noxious gases had continued to build up, the water in the ocean biome had turned acidic, and the site had been overrun by "crazy ants" and morning glories. A complete overhaul of oversight and operations was in the works. To the outside world, it was being cast as a restructuring. In truth, it was much more: The Biosphere was to be shut down indefinitely. Gold had been pink-slipped.

"Not the end of the world?" he said dejectedly. "I suppose not."

"Stop sulking," she snapped.

"Your sympathy is touching."

"Thank you. Don't forget, I'm out of a job too."

"Yeah, but I'm looking at the bigger picture. This could be a huge career black eye. It may not be as easy to line up the next gig as it was in the past. And we're not getting any younger. I thought we could make a go of it with the Biosphere."

Mrs. Gold's eyes narrowed, and she said nothing.

Just then the phone rang in their hotel room.

"Hello?" Gold said.

"Dr. Gold? It's me, Monica. Dirk and I just wanted to call to see how you were. We feel terrible about the Biosphere being shut down."

"Monica, you're a sweet girl," Gold said. "Your call means a lot to me. By the way, I know you kids were sneaking out for pizza."

"Dirk wants to speak with you, too," Monica said. "Don't worry, it's going to be alright."

"Thank you for the kind words," Gold said.

She handed Dirk the phone, and Dirk extended his best wishes before they both hung up.

Judy Gold took a break from pacing the room to look out the window. Gold joined his wife and looked out at the palm trees that ringed the hotel swimming pool.

Judy thought wistfully of Monstro.

∎

Angel had kissed his old life goodbye. What had possessed him to stay on Mars with Svetlana? Life on Mars *was* very relaxing, he had to admit. Did he miss everyone from the

Baby Doll? Fluffy? His Monday-night poker game? Yes. But there was more to life. And what of Svetlana? She was a dynamo. Was she crazy? They seemed perfectly suited to each other.

He watched her puttering about their apartment. How funny, he thought, that his quest to "reclaim" Julia had somehow led him here to Mars with a former model/cosmonaut sex maniac! It could be a lot worse. He had joined a Friday- night poker game with some of his new Buddhist friends on Mars, and had entered a billiards league with some of the same people. Then his thoughts turned to Julia, and everything seemed bittersweet.

∎

"It was an epiphany you had with Monstro in the Biosphere that first day," Bill observed.

"Yeah, I guess you could say that, now that I think about it," Cap said.

They sat on the patio of the Chateau Marmont. A few other luncheon guests sat nearby. The sky was relentlessly blue.

A short time later Morty joined them, and they introduced themselves. They made small talk for a few minutes, then Morty got down to business.

"I thought the treatment was interesting," Morty said. "But why is there a different name on it?"

"That's my pen name," Bill said.

"Oh. Okay. Tell me a little more about the story, the characters."

"It's the story of a guy and a whale that he chances to meet. Kind of an update of *Moby Dick*. Let's say *Moby Dick* meets *The Apartment*. A number of societal forces conspire to keep the two of them apart. The whale takes on a totemic quality," Bill said.

"Okay, it's the story of a quest. Does this guy have any love interests?" Morty asked.

"No, it's not that kind of story," Cap said with annoyance.

"Well, it's an interesting premise. I've visited the Biosphere, so the treatment caught my interest. I'm not sure we could sell our backers on this particular project. There's no real hook, no haymaker—nothing I think I can pitch with any success. But if you have other ideas in the future, I'd be interested in hearing about them."

"We've got lots of ideas," Bill said.

Morty smiled. The three of them sat talking enthusiastically for a few more minutes, then Morty took his leave.

■

Richard and Julia were having a quiet dinner alone at the Ivy. The conversation turned to Richard's script meeting the other day with Morty.

"So, what's the picture?" she asked.

"The Fountainhead."

"I love *The Fountainhead."*

"Morty wants me to play Howard Roark."

"Great. How about the female lead?"

"I think he's going to ask Patricia Neal to reprise the role she created."

"It just might work," Julia said sarcastically.

"Your name came up. But Morty thinks it would be a bad career move for us to keep playing opposite each other."

"Morty does, does he? So who do you see in the role? Some bimbo whose pants you can get into, no doubt," she snarled. She could feel herself starting to fly into an uncontrollable, jealous rage. She turned red with anger, and her eyes began to tear up.

"Julia, calm down." He could see a temper tsunami about to engulf the premises.

"I'm very calm," Julia said softly. She rose and yanked the tablecloth away, sending glassware, silverware and dishes flying. "Very calm," she muttered, and stormed out.

Richard smiled and tried to make the best of the situation, as everyone in the restaurant was now staring at him with a mixture of shock and sympathy. He shrugged, as if to say, "She does this all the time. I'm her long-suffering friend."

■

Monstro had had enough of captivity. It was time to return to the ocean. He eyed Cap, who was standing on the end of the jetty. Was Monstro prepared?

Cap knew this was goodbye, but he understood it was for the best. He also felt he and Monstro had developed a mutual respect and understanding. How had they ended up in the shallow waters off San Diego? Due to the Biosphere's closing, Monstro, like the Golds, was out of a job. Tearfully, Judy Gold had determined Monstro was now, finally, ready to be released.

Cap turned to Monstro.

"You watch yourself, big fella. I'm not going to be there to cover your back. There are a lot of mean fuckers out there."

Monstro nodded.

Cap continued. "Everything is so vast. Man's desires are petty by comparison. You are so big—bigger than life. Identity is complicated. Who are we? Do we have anything unique to offer that separates us from the crowd? Are we walking on a high wire with no one to catch us if we fall? Monstro, you're at the center of the universe with all the planets spinning around you on their axes. Only apart from society will your life find meaning. You exist on a solitary, sublime plane—in a world both ancient and futuristic. There, I've said my piece."

It was an emotional disquisition, and Monstro rather enjoyed it. He sensed that Cap was trying to articulate something grand beyond his ability to express. Then the great beast turned and with a swoosh of his giant tail plunged into the deep.